PULP
Literature

PULP Literature

PULP LITERATURE PRESS

Issue No. 33, Spring 2023

Publisher: Pulp Literature Press; Managing Editor: Jennifer Landels; Senior Editor: Mel Anastasiou; Acquisitions Editor: Genevieve Wynand; Poetry Editors: Daniel Cowper & Emily Osborne; Assistant Editors: Brooklynn Hook, Nik Kos, Melisa Gruger, Jeya Thiessen, Sierra Louie, Ellen Spacey; Copy Editor: Amanda Bidnall; Proofreader: Sierra Louie; Graphic Design: Amanda Bidnall; Cover Design: Kate Landels; Subscriptions & Advertising: Brooklynn Hook. For advertising rates, direct inquiries to info@pulpliterature.com.

Cover painting, *Ups and Downs* by M St James. Artwork for 'Dragon's Greed' by Anat Rabkin. All other illustrations by Mel Anastasiou.

Pulp Literature: ISSN 2292-2164 (Print), ISSN 2292-2172 (Digital), Issue No. 38, Spring 2023.

Published quarterly by Pulp Literature Press, 21955 16 Ave, Langley, BC, Canada V2Z IK5, pulpliterature.com, at $15.00 per copy. Annual subscription $50.00 in Canada, $72.00 in continental USA, $86.00 elsewhere. Printed in Victoria, BC, Canada, by First Choice Books / Victoria Bindery. Copyright © 2023 Pulp Literature Press. All stories and works of art copyright © 2023 their authors as per bylines.

Pulp Literature Press gratefully acknowledges the support of the Canada Council for the Arts.

Pulp Literature is a proud member of the Magazine Association of BC and Magazines Canada.

TABLE OF CONTENTS

FROM THE PULP LIT PULPIT

Again, for the First Time

Three years ago, I wrote my first editorial for *Pulp Literature*. It was for Issue 27, a summer release. As I was writing, it was March 2020, and we (the global we) were staring down a new virus, the cut of whose swathe we couldn't predict and wouldn't fathom for a long while. At the time, though, I wondered if the virus was even worth mentioning. Would it, and all that it entailed, still be a thing when the issue went to press? Well, as we all know, it was—and still is—a thing.

Truth be told, I wondered once more, here on my post-pandemic perch in early 2023, whether it was even worth mentioning again. But the eternal optimist in me suggested that now might be just the right time to offer a follow-up, a bookend of sorts. Because, although so very much was lost, some was gained. Absent

regular contact (except, of course, for those ever-present Zoom meetings), we realized we *do* need each other—quite a lot, in fact.

Folks explored long-quieted hobbies and discovered new interests, writing chief among them. Publications saw an unprecedented (ah yes, *that* word again!) number of submissions. Unable to share physical space, people shared their stories. And it wasn't just that we all suddenly had more time to think; we had more time to think things through.

Like generations past, indelibly marked by their own age, we'll never be able to fully wipe clean our pandemic goggles. The world is a fragile place, and we are fragile creatures. And as I learned in 2020, we may not always read the future accurately, but we can continue to step into it one day—one page—at a time.

As I said then, we hope these words find you safe and well and reassured in knowing that as one season ends, a new one always begins.

~*Genevieve Wynand*

*I*N THIS ISSUE

Ups and Downs by cover artist **M St James** offers us a feathered familiar to guide our way through this issue, starting with 'The Caged Bird Sings in a Darkness of Its Own Creation' by feature author **Richard Thomas**.

Winged creatures fly to the rescue in 'Olympian' by **FJ Bergmann**, 'Andouille' by **Mike Carson**, and 'Dragon's Greed' by **Sherilyn Moreton** and **Anat Rabkin**. But human rescues miss the mark in 'All Our Swains Commend Her' by **Mitchell Toews** and 'The Least of Myself' by **Sylvia Leong**.

The winner and runner-up of the Raven Short Story Contest alight, carrying memories and regrets in 'Revolutions' by **Cate Sandilands** and 'Foam' by **Alison Stevenson**, while 'Waffles and Strawberries' by **Susan Alexander** shows us a present that fails to live up to the past.

Finally, leave the known world behind and take charge of your adventure into the unknown with **Melanie Marttila**'s 'Psychopomps Are Us', **Mel Anastasiou**'s 'Stella Ryman vs the Board', and 'The Shepherdess: The Trail of Yellow Roses' by **JM Landels**.

PULP
Literature

FANTASTIC
FRESH
FICTION

www.pulpliterature.com

THE CAGED BIRD SINGS IN A DARKNESS OF ITS OWN CREATION

Richard Thomas

Richard Thomas is the award-winning author of four novels, four short story collections, and 170 stories in print, and he is the editor of four anthologies. He has been nominated for the Bram Stoker, Shirley Jackson, Thriller, and Audie awards. Visit what-doesnotkillme.com for more information.

© 2023, Richard Thomas

The Caged Bird Sings in a Darkness of Its Own Creation

In the northernmost reaches of the Silverpine Forest, past the lumber mill, east of the abandoned mine, just this side of Devil's Gorge, there is a hut. It's nothing special, really, scraps of wood and sheet metal held together with rumour and rusty nails, a roof made out of old billboards, a hint of a cereal ad peeking through, and a splash of red—a faded logo barely visible.
How is it still standing after all this time? That can be debated.

Perhaps it was built in the shadow of a huge oak tree that shades the structure, protecting it, the occasional acorns raining down on the wood and metal roof creating a ripple of percussion in the otherwise quiet forest. Maybe it's the animal fat that is slathered over the frame: the sinew wrapped around one board after another, dried creating a bond that might be cemented even further tomorrow or the next day. Or it might be something else entirely—an illusion, some sort of glimmer of technology rippling under the building, a line of gold running through the tiny house, as if a motherboard had been pressed into the rotting wood, a surge of electricity running over it all then fading as the sun pushes through the dense foliage. Whatever is happening here, the old man standing in the doorway holds a flickering presence, daunting in the shadow and void he creates but vulnerable in his sickly thin appearance, an old flannel shirt barely covering his pale flesh and bony arms, dirty jeans leading down to black boots that are grotesquely oversized, the only bit of joy his shockingly bright hair in a rainbow of colours, as well as a red bulbous nose. He grabs the sphere and rips it off, leaving behind a gap where a fleshy proboscis must have once resided, flinging the spongy crimson ball to the forest floor, where it bounces into a pile of leaves and disappears. He turns and heads back into the residence, the nose back on his face, a bit of magic here, the illusion continuing.

When the acorns fall again, he begins weeping, muttering the name of a long-lost love under his breath, his sobs turning into a rasping cough and then to something darker — something wet. Other random noises emanate from the hut — sometimes from him, and sometimes from the dozens of jars that line the walls, shelves full of clear glass, and a curiosity of items. As he rolls about on the cot, transferring white paste and powder to the dirty sheets and blankets, the tension in his stomach builds until he leans over and vomits up a long stream of tangled balloons in a shocking mix of rubber iridescence. Mixed in with the puddle of primary colours is a smattering of glitter, a few chunks of glistening meat, sawdust, and a handful of marbles, that go rolling across the floor.

In the jars, there is much more.

A tiny heart, somehow still beating, floats in a yellowing liquid. Next to it, a bowl filled with yo-yos, the strings crusted with brown stains, a meaty smell lifting off of the faded toys. In a large glass mason jar, there is nothing but hair — long blonde strands, several puffs of dark, curly tightness, and brown clippings in a number of lengths, all mixed together.

It doesn't stop there.

A little glass music box is filled with glittering metal — rings and necklaces, in silver and gold, some plastic, some onyx, all inlaid with memory, and trace amounts of DNA. Next to that is a large clear vase filled with toothbrushes in a variety of colours — some brand-new or nearly that, others worn down, the bristles frayed, handles bent and faded, the edges worn away from use. There is a jar filled with flickering fireflies humming and buzzing in the night. A clay bowl is overflowing with little rubber balls that mix and mingle, vibrating with hate and sorrow. A gilded cage toward the back of the little room is filled to bursting with tiny birds in a cacophony of pigmentation — chirping red, twittering blue, gasping black into the encroaching night. There is so much pain gathered here, and the sobbing form lying on the floor knows exactly what he's done, the role he has played in all this sadness.

As the darkness settles in around the humble abode, the hut goes quiet, a crinkling of leaves buried under snapping sticks, the tall shadows outside standing in a semi-circle around the building, their long necks and slender arms extending in ways that are hard to rationalize. Six of these elongated figures hold court in this desolate forest, chittering to each other, a dull glow seeping from their myriad eyes. Their skeletal frames rise nearly to the tops of the encroaching trees, their oval heads brushing up against the green leaves, bent over in worship or perhaps just to get a closer look.

Inside, he stirs, and swallows with some effort, a coil of madness unfurling in his gut, the time for his departure at hand. He has played host for so many years now, and a series of black-and-white photos unfurl in front of his watering eyes: cracking jokes in grade school and then sent to the corner of the room, a dunce cap on top of his head; sitting at a bar, sipping beer and telling stories as the women eased in closer, the laughter slipping from their blushed lips, their eyes crinkling with happiness; the television cameras bearing down on his face as he cavorted for their amusement, the children at his feet filled with wonder, the ache in his gut swirling around and around.

He knows they are here now, returned. But the price he had to pay, it seems exorbitant, out of balance with what he has reaped, what has been sowed. In the beginning, there was no length he wouldn't go to in order to get back what he loved. But over time the cost grew and expanded, one more task, one more item, until there was no turning back.

In for a penny, in for a pound.

And that pound of flesh has been taken. Over and over again.

To what end?

Eventually, it was inverted. Not the death of one for the good of many, but the opposite — the death of many for the good of one. Or the few.

Or so he thought.

As the ripples of his actions scattered across the globe and beyond, the man with the funny shoes and the sparkling eyes wept into his trembling hands. And the worm in his belly squirmed with a heady anticipation.

They were going home.

Somewhere in the dark, millions of miles away and yet entirely on top of this event, so very distant and yet, essentially, filling the same space, a massive pair of hands is busy creating. They are moving quickly, a blur, and yet, upon closer inspection, moving infinitely slow. There is a vast tableau in front of this being, spilling out in every direction, the great presence surrounded by satellites of life, motes of dark energy, electric fields riddled with animation — so many sights, sounds, and smells.

Taking a deep breath in, it exhales into its fists, a flurry of feathers circling like a fixed tornado in blue and white, spinning round and round, forming a murmuration of life and movement. Off to the left, several hundred bluebirds scatter into the never-ending darkness.

The hands reach out into the ether and conjure up a handful of dirt, packing it in tightly then reaching up as if to find a lost memory, pulling twigs and berries out of nothingness, pushing the wood and red juice together, tugging here and there, eventually opening to spill out a herd of deer, some with antlers budding, others fully formed, the creatures standing on tepid legs then dashing off in excitement and fear.

Holding one giant hand over the other, its fingertips sprinkle dust and droplets of water over the cupped hand below, and a squirming starts to spool and twist in the palm of the mighty being — dark green, the smell of algae and seaweed swimming up into the air, one tentacle after another pushing out of the mass, growing faster and faster until it overflows the hand that holds it. With a sigh and a squinting eye, a handful of sharp teeth are shoved into the wriggling creature, an undulating mass of tiny bulbous eyes crammed into the middle of the wriggling, rippling mass. When it surges again, it is released into the darkness, a singular monstrosity destined for a distant planet, an ocean with unlimited depths.

This has been happening for a long time; it is happening now; it will happen for all of eternity.

It bends over and snaps its fingers, lighting a fire at its fingertips, the flames licking at what must be flesh, trying to cajole the flickering light, a difficult task. The smell of meat cooking fills the air, an earthy wood burning sweet and smoky, as the sinuous form leaps out of the gesticulating hands before it is complete, before it becomes what was planned. But this is life, this is creation: intention, and then chaos.

With a long, steady blow, a wind leaves its massive lips, a funnel of cool air whirling about, swirling and taking on mass, long, leathery wings extending. The creator narrows its gaze, and shakes its head, trying to manipulate the shape as a beak elongates and talons scratch at the air—first one winged beast, then two, doubling in number, released with frustration, scales and needles spilling behind them, this experiment another failure.

Only two, it thinks. It could have been worse.

And in its anger it makes a fist, pounding what would have been a table, a surface, if such things existed here, but it finds resistance nonetheless. And in that singular gesture, a spark of atoms spills out of its clenched fingers, a sickly yellow cancer spreading out and over the trembling knot of digits, the tiny flashes of light and oozing sickness taking on a microscopic form, expanding and then contracting, breeding in and of itself, and when its presence is noticed, fully formed, it disappears into the ether, death wandering out to claim its stake—seeking out weakness and feeding on misery.

It pauses for a moment, this rippling form, taking in a deep breath, its many forms shifting as a wave of emotions washes over it. Calm, collected, legs folded, hand on knees. Then its head tilts back, its eyes ablaze, as a deep laughter builds up from inside tinted flesh, feet to hooves, followed by nubs bursting from a cracking skull. It inhales, and its pale flesh expands. It runs a hand over its bald head and expanding belly, a gleam in its eyes, a smile upon its fleshy face. And then its arms double, then triple, a third eye upon its forehead, a glitter of gold sprinkling down like rain from a cloud, a clash of cymbals, and then silence.

It was all things; it is all things; it will be all things.

It goes back to work.

It focuses for a moment on mankind, and, pulling a sack of what might be seen as marbles out of the darkness, it spills the assortment of spirits upon a false ground. In a flurry of activity, the shapes ping off of each other—a clacking sound, and then a great sigh, a moan of contentment, and then a cry of fear and loss—as it manipulates the dozens of entities with a deft touch and a sharp eye. They shiver into life. A push here, a pinch there, a whisper to this handful cupped up close to its mouth and then scattered back on the floor. A sparking of blue and green is followed by a flash of red and orange, a singular white orb spinning and hovering all by itself, while a solitary black sphere sits in one place, vibrating with anger and vengeance.

It scatters the bulk of these new beings out into the universe, some seeking light, others wallowing in the endless darkness. It picks up the only one left, the obsidian globule, and brings it close to its trembling eyes. The hard shell is cold in its grip, but a shallow pulse of warm light is buried within, that sparks white, sparks yellow, flashes a momentary glow that makes its creator smile.

It is given a name now, it is shown how to bring joy to the world, the children, it is told of how other life might exist far beyond its reach, and it warns of how such power and knowledge might corrupt, eventually.

And then it is set free.

It is born unto the earth.

It will hear laughter in the form of innocent children.

And it will make decisions — both horrible and inspired.

Such is life.

At a very young age Edward Carnby had the first in a series of visions that would transform and define his life. And because he believed what he saw, these moments had great power — to alter his future, and those of the people around him as well. Some say that the tall shadows were nothing more than a fever, a flu from when he was lost in the woods, a sickness that caused the boy to lie in bed for weeks on end, a cancer in his bones that would cause a slight limp in his gait.

Others can confirm what was there in the forest — too many concrete details kept in their fluttering minds, in metal tins at the back of closets, in safe deposit boxes, the keys rusty and lost long ago. There is no real way to explain away the tiny knobs, levers, and bits of heavy black rock that were melted into odd shapes. Found downstream, in the backs of caves and buried deep in an assortment of fields, the materials they were made of could not be found anywhere on earth.

But there may be a third explanation here as well.

Three moments, three wishes.

What happened?

At the age of twelve, Eddie used to wander the woods in search of arrowheads, empty wasp nests, tree bark curled into sheets of paper, and bright blue robins' eggs — some intact, others cracked open and empty. He was fascinated by the offerings nature presented to him. He might find a field filled with budding flowers in yellow and purple, with hints of red. He might see in the ponds, lakes, and creeks a variety of silver-backed fish swimming in schools, some with a wash of shimmer and a stripe of colour: perch, trout, bass, and carp. And sometimes he found death — that egg cracked open with a bit of fluff and bone inside, a singular eye gazing up; a skeleton riddled with a sour stench inside a thorny bush, the red of its fur faded and damp; now and then just a splash of blood and a bit of sinew, nothing left but a stain, with buzzing flies marking the expiration.

It all fascinated him: life, death, and everything in between.

It was on one of these hikes that he found the shadow child, a thin trail of smoke leading up into the sky, a dent in the earth, and a smattering of flickering metal across a field of puffing dandelions. There was an echo in his head, his ears filled with the sound of cascading water, and at the same time, it was entirely quiet.

When a baby bird falls from a nest, the story is that it shouldn't be touched, that any kind of interaction with human flesh will taint the creature, the mother bird pecking it to death, sensing only trouble and danger. This is not true. But that doesn't mean the action goes unnoticed, that the bird is not aware, that the gesture is not recorded — for future action, good or bad.

Of course Eddie bent over and touched the clear gel, the shadow pulsing within it, the strange form lying prostrate in the dirt, a hum of some machine winding down, the smell of oil and plastic burning. It was unlike anything he had ever seen.

He thought that there were words slipping from the form, some sort of plea. As he knelt in the field, in the itching grass and moist soil next to the fading silhouette, it was in his nature to touch it, his hand slipping through the glistening form, a gasp from them both, a ringing of bells, a stinging across his flesh, a triggering of some alarm, his body suddenly covered in a sheen of sweat. It was electric, it was liquid, it was a marking in self-defence by the creature lying beneath him.

Pulling his hand back, the shadow dissipated, the remaining gelatinous shape seeping into the earth, Eddie's hand held up high in front of his flickering gaze—glowing red, then absorbing into his flesh, around him the metal and plastic smoking, melting—reduced to ash, the wind scattering the detritus to the far corners of the field.

Standing up, it was all gone. No smoke, no fragments or evidence—just an empty field, the sound of wildlife slipping back into focus. The boy swallowed hard and turned in a circle. He walked the field, pushing aside long grass, sending dandelion seeds flying but nothing more. He was unable to see the remnants, his vision distorted forever, altered in crucial ways. It would be much later when others found the strange remains.

He looked to the sky, asking for an explanation, wishing for something more. He was eager to learn, to grow, to comprehend.

That would be a mistake.

Later that night he would take a very long time to fall asleep.

The next day the memory would fade, and he would forget it had ever happened.

Mostly.

Almost.

But not quite.

It would be twelve years down the road at the ripe old age of twenty-four that he would revisit this moment in an entirely different way.

Standing in an alleyway outside a local bar, smoking a cigarette and thinking about a girl that was inside playing pool, Eddie noticed a gathering of shadows down by the trash cans and dumpsters. For a moment he thought it was some local boys he'd had trouble with in the past — simple folk who had no aspirations, who were often offended by his lengthy conversations, and for whom the attention of blondes and brunettes alike stirred up something close to a primal, territorial rage. But it wasn't those kids.

In an instant, Eddie was on his knees, one hand held up, inspected by the shifting shadows, a glow spilling into the night. His mouth opened as if to scream, but nothing came out. His vision was watery, *shimmering*, a darkness descending upon him like a ratty blanket, the smell of smoke and burning plastic filling the air, and before he passed out, a sharp pain invading his gut. They would hardly leave a mark. The only evidence of this moment was a tiny red dot — something a mosquito, or spider, might make.

When he wakes, there is only one thought in his head.

Wait.

Don't go.

Hold on.

It is fading fast, the memory, but he has glimpsed something extraordinary, and he wants to see more.

And he will. In time.

In the coming weeks he will get sick — a fever of 103; a horrible rash that creeps across his skin in mottled hues; nausea that causes him to vomit into the toilet with a violent upheaval, the blood and mucus dotted with tiny flecks of metal, all triggering some deeper knowledge that he is afraid to truly recognize.

And then it is gone.

The hosting is complete.

His work is only beginning.

The third time, ten years later, will cement their relationship as he sits in front of a mirror, putting on his makeup, the lights on the dressing table bright yellow, a smile splitting his face as he glues on the red nose, pulls the wig on tight, a wriggle of anxiety in his gut.

There is a woman, Gina.

She is everything he has ever wanted in a woman: long blonde hair, sparkling blue eyes, curves hidden behind modest dresses, and an easy smile that fills his gut with mating butterflies.

For Edward, this is the love of his life, a relationship that has bloomed over the last couple of years through cups of coffee, dancing at local watering holes, seeing her out in the audience at his shows, smiling with glee.

For Gina, these are merely coincidences: a Venti Mocha on the way to work with a nod to the strange pudgy man in the corner booth; a night out with the girls at the only place to dance for miles; a visit to the television station to laugh at the clown, a bit of a local celebrity—kept at a safe distance, after all.

In the shadows of his closet, there is a murmuring, a beckoning, and Edward, soon to be Krinkles (and *only* Krinkles) answers. He stands in the back of the tiny space and nods his head. He listens to what is offered. And it is set in motion.

It will spill out into the future.

Look close, and see what it becomes.

See what you want to see, as Krinkles does.

The truth is a slippery fish.

When the tired old man leaves the hut once again, they are waiting. Patient for so long. With all of their technology, their abilities, and their desire, they cannot walk the earth in shadow, for the eyes of the planet are upon them. They have been seen, and they have been hurt.

But their work here is done now.

And in a blink, they vanish.

In a distant laboratory, the worm is removed under bright lights in a sterile environment. It is placed into a container where later it will be downloaded, dissected, and documented for the benefit of them all.

In the living room of a quaint little cottage, just on the edge of an entirely different set of woods — not far from a rippling stream filled with colourful fish and a field overflowing with blooming flowers and dancing grass — Edward sits and smiles. He rocks in his chair, sipping a cup of chamomile tea, comfortable in his soft new flannel shirt, his faded jeans, the windows open, birdsong slipping in, the television quietly playing black-and-white shows from his childhood.

He laughs.

When the woman enters the room, he takes the plate with the ham and cheese sandwich on rye, a bit of Dijon mustard slathered on there, rippled potato chips, and a dill pickle on the side. She kisses his forehead, and he thanks her, saying her name. It's a recognizable name. When she enters the kitchen her skin flickers, the tapestry that is tightly wrapped over her metal frame, plastic shell, and coloured wiring dissipating for a moment.

On a wall to the left of Edward is a large mirror. There are days he stares at it, thinking he sees a shimmer. But most of the time he is content. He thinks of his childhood, his career, the woman he loves, and while parts of his life feel thin at times, a headache forming if he looks at it too closely, he is grateful.

Behind that mirror there may only be a wall.

Behind that mirror there might be men watching Edward, taking notes, nodding their heads, and smiling in the darkness, their work a success.

Behind that mirror there could be elongated shadows stretching to the ceiling, hunched over, chirping in the gloom, eyes glowing.

There may not be a mirror at all.

Edward may lie dying in that first forest, his dark deeds finally absorbing the last of his humanity, death a welcome respite.

The jars, the bowls, the DNA — perhaps they were stolen in secret, nobody harmed (especially not the children), saving an alien race from a plethora of sickness and disease.

Or maybe it's something much worse.

In the expanding corners of a never-ending universe, the creator smiles. Its work here is done.

FEATURE INTERVIEW

Richard Thomas

Pulp Literature: *In the opening scene of the 'The Caged Bird Sings in a Darkness of Its Own Creation', I felt like I was entering a land of curiosities, a museum of the strange. Surprisingly, it made me think of the little totems and icons I have arranged ever so carefully on the eye-level shelf at my writing desk. What icons do you surround yourself with? What takes pride of place on your altar of inspiration and craft?*

RT: Wow, what a great question. I totally surround myself with art, icons, sculptures, carvings, rocks, you name it. In my office I have some *Blade Runner* items, some petrified wood from our travels across the country, a black raven sculpture from a Ukrainian artist, a bunch of weird Funko Pop! dudes, carved birds, metal steampunk rabbits and turtles, Studio Ghibli characters, etc. All of these items make me stop and think, or smile, or just appreciate the artistry of some talented individual. Glad you liked the opening to that story. It's supposed to be items that at first are just common, even associated with kids, but the more you look at them, the weirder and more sinister it gets. A jar full of colourful toothbrushes? How bright and varied. Oh wait, look at all of this HAIR in a jar over here and a bunch of dirty yo-yos. It gets weird, fast.

PL: *In creating Edward, did you work in layers — person inside clown, worm inside person, creator close enough to touch both yet cosmologically distant — or was the process entirely something else?*

RT: Believe it or not, I've never written a clown story — in fifteen years of dark fiction — and then I wrote two in the same year: this story, and 'Clown Face'. For 'Caged Bird' there was a built universe, some history already there, and by the time I was included in the project, some stories were already written. So I started with what was there, and then pushed outward into the weird. I like what you said here — person inside the clown, worm inside the person. There are some interesting visuals in this story that are uniquely alien — in every sense of the word. And I wanted the ending, as well as that creator scene, to really make the reader stop and think about what they were seeing here. What is real, and what is imagined? There are numerous ways to interpret that ending. And Edward, really. Typically we create a three-act play in our structures — beginning, middle, and end. I wanted to break that format with the creator scene because I'm a maximalist and writing a lot of new-weird and hopepunk lately. I kept asking myself, "How did he get here? How was he created?" And that scene helped to explain some of the larger, more cosmic aspects to his story.

PL: *Could you tell us more about how hopepunk plays into your work?*

RT: Sure. Hopepunk is essentially the opposite of grimdark. I think my desire to put more hope into my writing came about during Covid. I mean, so many people were dying. It was intense. And I just couldn't write bleak stories with sad endings that put the reader through hell and then everything went dark. It was too much for me. So this goes back perhaps five years or so. In fact, most of the stories in my collection, *Spontaneous Human Combustion,* lean into that—not the idea of *combustion* (bursting into flames) but the duality of human nature, the spontaneous *human* combustion, how we release ourselves, how we hide our inner demons, and how we exorcise them. Sure, sometimes the horror wins, but in many of the stories in that collection there is vengeance, there is justice, a balancing of the scales, and hope.

PL: *You sit on both sides of the editorial desk. How does your work as a writer influence your work as an editor? What does the editor in you want your writerly self to remember?*

RT: It's all connected, right? I start as a *reader*—all my life, with a lot of Stephen King beginning in high school. And as King has said, in order to be a writer you must do two things: you must read, and you must write. So I start from a place of entertainment, pleasure, and imagination. It's body, mind, and soul for me—entertaining, getting you to think, and moving you, emotionally. When I write, I try not to edit at first. Though I may sit and chew on a story for days, weeks, even months before I actually start writing. Over the years, my instincts have gotten better, and all of the things I've been taught in various classes and in my MFA become subconscious actions. I think less, and create more. But I'm very aware of the process—narrative hooks, inciting incidents, internal and external conflicts, rising tension, climax, resolution and change, denouement and epiphany. The Freytag Triangle is always close at hand. I'm not precious with my work, and having published some 175 stories, I can tell when it's working and when it's not. So while I start from a point of creativity, the editor's hat is usually sitting right here, as well.

PL: *Your website name, whatdoesnotkillme, implies an ellipsis of sorts, and suggests to me something fundamental to the submission cycle — surviving rejection. Though perhaps I am projecting! Are we to infer the 'makes me stronger' is related to honing our craft, or is there something else going on here?*

RT: For sure, you're not wrong here LOL. When I write, I tap into everything I've ever seen, done, suffered through, accomplished, felt, you name it. There are horrible nightmares in those moments and also wonder and magic, success. I use both. I try to open up on the page, be vulnerable, expose myself and the universal truths I've experienced, and then try to make it unique. Getting through all of that, rejection in the world, rejection with our work — you get stronger and learn, or you live in denial and repeat the same mistakes. I've had stories rejected twenty, forty, one hundred times and then land with professional markets, get nominated for awards. Nietzsche is a philosopher I studied in college, and some of what he had to say really spoke to me. It's the idea of being stronger where you're broken, the bones knitting back together in strength. Surviving and learning. Being able to adapt. If you don't fight for your stories, as the writer of these stories, who else is going to do that for you? Nobody. Sure, an agent, if you're shopping a novel, but for the individual stories, it's usually YOU. There is a deep joy in finally breaking through to a market after years of submitting. I've been lucky to get into *Cemetery Dance* several times, and each one of those stories was rejected twenty, thirty, forty times first — sometimes taking more than a year to land. It's tough out there. But if you put in the work, if you really give it your all, workshop your stories, and fight for them—you'll have a good chance of succeeding.

PL: *On this long and winding writerly path, what keeps you hungry?*

RT: Every time I sit down to write, I do that by trying to create something special. Whether I'm invited into a project, or sending out my work cold to a variety of publications, I want to do my best work. There are quite a few markets that I haven't broken into, so I keep them in mind; they keep me hungry. I got into the *Best Horror of the Year* in the past, but it was for a co-written story, so I'd like to get in again for a solitary work. And of course there are the awards and film rights and other ways of getting recognized. Mostly it's telling the stories. I'm constantly inspired by what I see out in the world. Horrified, as well. I love writing stories that connect with readers. And of late, that means more hope in my dark fiction. If I can help one person to get through the night, to feel a little bit less alone, less of a freak or outsider, then it's worth it.

PL: *'The Caged Bird Sings in a Darkness of Its Own Creation' is so incredibly visually complex. Any thoughts of turning it into a graphic novel?*

RT: I hadn't thought about that, no. But I'd be open to it for sure. I appreciate the kind words. As a maximalist writer, for me setting and sensory detail are important, so the visuals of seeing the clown in that cabin, the things in the woods, the creator scene, as well as the ending—yeah, I see it well, it's rather cinematic to me. That's the way I like to write.

PL: *Thank you for making the time to speak with us. Before we go, tell us: what are you working on now?*

RT: My agent is shopping my fourth book, *Incarnate*. It's a sin-eater, arctic horror novel inspired by *The Thing*, *The Terror*, the work of Stephen Graham Jones and Brian Evenson, all with a dash of *The Giver*. Fingers crossed we have good news on that soon, this year. Other than that, just a few stories here and there, one ('Battle Not With Monsters') out in *Cemetery Dance* any day now, and of course my fourth short story collection, *Spontaneous Human Combustion*, came out last year; hoping it makes a few ballots. Much appreciation for the excellent questions here. Thank you for your interest and support. Means a lot.

$\mathcal{S}$ELECT BIBLIOGRAPHY

FICTION

Spontaneous Human Combustion (Turner Publishing, 2022); story collection

Tribulations (Cemetery Dance / Crystal Lake, 2016); story collection

The Soul Standard (Dzanc Books, 2016); novella

Breaker (Random House Alibi, 2016); novel

Disintegration (Random House Alibi, 2015); novel

Staring Into the Abyss: Stories (Kraken Press, 2013); story collection

Herniated Roots: Stories (Snubnose Press, 2012); story collection

Transubstantiate (Otherworld Publications, 2010); novel

As Editor

Gamut Magazine (2016–2018)

Dark House Press (2014–2016)

The Lineup: 20 Provocative Women Writers (Black Lawrence Press, 2015)

Exigencies (Dark House Press, 2015)

Burnt Tongues, with Chuck Palahniuk and Dennis Widmyer
(Medallion, 2014 / Turner Publishing, 2020)

Smokelong Quarterly (June 2014)

The New Black (Dark House Press, 2014)

New Madrid (Summer 2010)

STELLA RYMAN VS THE BOARD

Mel Anastasiou

Mel Anastasiou *writes the Fairmount Manor Mysteries, the Hertfordshire Pub Mysteries, and the Monument Studios Mysteries. Winner of a Literary Titan Gold award and longlisted for the Leacock Medal, Mel is also the author of two illustrated thirty-day workbooks on story structure: the steampunk-themed* The Writer's Boon Companion *and* The Writer's Friend and Confidante. *For news on published and upcoming new works, visit her website, melanastasiou.wordpress.com.*

Octogenarian sleuth Stella Ryman returns for her twelfth adventure with 'Stella Ryman vs the Board', wherein Stella works to thwart the top dogs of the machineries of institution, Fairmount's Board of Directors, while she investigates a perplexing care home mystery. You can find the first two full-length books, Stella Ryman and the Fairmount Manor Mysteries *and* The Labours of Mrs Stella Ryman, *at pulpliterature.com and from most booksellers. Book 3,* Stella Ryman and the Search for Thelma Hu, *comes out in 2023 from Pulp Literature Press.*

© 2023, Mel Anastasiou

FAIRMOUNT MANOR

Stella Ryman vs the Board

Fairmount Manor residents marked the arrival of spring more out of faith than observation. True, everybody could see out the windows, but the hedges around the care home needed trimming, so in most areas of Fairmount, residents had to imagine for themselves that the morning sun shone down outside the care home upon houses, streets, and alleyways.

A librarian who had for decades adjusted and inked her date stamp did not lightly suffer chronological uncertainty. Stella had grown tired of asking the Nameless Dear care workers what day it was, for even they often didn't know, and then they made a meal out of finding it out. She had moved to a far better system. She lay in wait behind her bedroom door for Ollie to step out of the emergency exit into the garden for his first smoke break of the day. When she heard the door lever clack shut behind him, she crept out and checked the date on his task clipboard, which hung on the handle of his yellow cleaning trolley. In this way she had learned it was the sixth of May, and furthermore that Fairmount's Board of Directors was visiting this morning. Satisfying as this inside knowledge was, it couldn't compare with living a real life outside Fairmount. She wished she might experience May's spring sunshine directly by stepping outside the door of her own sweet house, which she had sold for the funds that, along with her teacher's pension, paid her way here at the care home. Here, where she was not allowed to step outside the building on her own.

She shook herself. There was no time this morning for home-sickness, longings for direct sunshine, or curiosity about the expected visit from the Board of Directors. For today, like every day, Stella had her duties to perform: a series of before-breakfast missions that were both useful and clandestine.

As usual, she began her rounds in Fern Corridor, where she knocked on Ruby's door. Ruby was unlikely to answer, as she was very hard of hearing, but civilized beings knocked, even in Fairmount Manor. It even mattered more here at Fairmount, where doors were not to be locked, or at least not locked by inmates. Inmates? No, *residents*. Fairmount Manor was not a prison. Not at all. Although, she noted, with more bitterness than she usually permitted herself, Fairmount did have a warden, *viz.* Mrs Perdita Warren, Director. The well-supervised children at the elementary school where Stella used to teach had enjoyed more freedom of movement than the Warden permitted her.

Soldier on, Stella.

She knocked again on Ruby's door and then let herself into the room. There, as most mornings, she got Ruby out of bed and dressed. Not long before, Stella had found Ruby naked and shivering in her chair, waiting for a care worker to dress her for breakfast. For some reason, whether random, geographical, or alphabetical, Ruby was always the last resident to receive care worker help before breakfast, and no amount of pleading by Stella had served to move Ruby up the list. This apparent unfairness infuriated her, but she knew in her heart that every resident on the care workers' morning assistance list was in serious need of help. So Stella dressed Ruby each morning. It was a little unsettling that Ruby believed her to be one of Fairmount's more senior employees. But what harm? None. Except that Stella, as a career teacher and school librarian, was a union woman, and worried sometimes that she was violating care workers' rights.

Stella tied Ruby's favourite red scarf in an ascot knot around her fragile neck. "Now you're all set for royalty this morning, Ruby."

"Stella, what is it like to be young like you?" Ruby marvelled. "Think of it. I used to be young myself."

"Now, Ruby, remember I'm older than you," Stella said. It wasn't true, but saying so always cheered Ruby. Stella wished her a good breakfast and darted out along the corridor before the real care worker assigned to Fern Corridor caught her dressing the residents.

With breakfast time still some minutes off, Stella slinked from door to door towards Dottie's room. En route she passed the Director's office and noted that the empty secretary's desk was missing from its spot outside the office. The Warden hadn't had a secretary for months, which was odd enough in itself; but now another piece of excellent mahogany furniture had vanished. This was an ongoing mystery, but all she'd discovered so far was that, if Thelma was correct in her valuation, the missing pieces of furniture were worth quite a lot of money.

Also of interest was a mysteriously well-dressed elderly man slouched in a folding wheelchair next to where the secretary's desk used to be. The man was asleep, and his chair sat parked at an ill-considered angle with one front wheel jammed against the wall of the Warden's office. Might this be a new resident, then? Careful not to disturb him, Stella turned his chair to face the corridor, so that he could at least look about when he woke up. When she set the wheelchair's brake, he opened his eyes, snorted thrice, and blinked up at her.

Stella said, "You'll be fine. It takes a few days to get used to things at Fairmount."

He didn't answer, and his stare was so uncertain that she wondered whether he was aware of his surroundings at all.

She added, "There's toast and marmalade for breakfast." He looked to her like a marmalade man.

She smiled, straightened the lapel of his top-notch linen jacket, and hurried onwards. When she reached Dottie's room in Fern Corridor, she found her, as usual, standing outside her closed door with her back pressed up against it.

Dottie said, "Hello, Stella. I don't have a cat. It's not allowed."

Stella said cheerfully, "I'll bet you wish you had a cat, though."

"I do wish it." Dottie peered past Stella along the empty corridor. "Cats are lovely. So loyal if you only understand them properly."

"Sure. I'd do anything for a cat myself." Stella fumbled in her pocket and pulled out a paper napkin with tuna fish in it. The fishy aroma arose from the napkin and filled this little area of Fairmount. It so happened that Stella had been saving this napkin full of tuna fish since lunchtime the day before, under the waste bin in her washroom, and she would be happy to be rid of it.

She held out the napkin to Dottie. "Be careful, and wash your hands afterwards. It's starting to turn."

Dottie took the napkin and peered inside it. "Thank you, Stella. I like it best when it goes a little off." She narrowed her eyes like the cat she professed not to keep, backed into her room, and pulled the door shut.

Stella pressed her ear against the door. She heard the tiny mew of feline appreciation from Dottie's cat Percy. She nodded sharply to herself. Fairmount Manor rooms were small, pets not allowed, and furthermore Ollie the care worker was a demon with institutional mops and dusters in every resident's bedroom. But there was only one of him, and many bedrooms. Thus far the secret of Percy endured. How did Dottie keep Ollie from barging in and smelling cat? Stella didn't know. She was longing to find out, and she would find out. But not today. Mysteries were to be savoured, not consumed.

Stella moved along the corridor towards the activities hall and past its gaping maw of a door. Her personal hell lay within: the hell of bridge tourneys and healthy movement classes. This morning, Stella wasn't looking for hell. She was looking for Theo Longbourne. Her friend Theo walked Fairmount's corridors all day long, only pausing to escort Stella and Sally from the Greek Chorus to meals, and alternating his attention between each of them. Reciprocally, Stella had lately shouldered a secret duty of her own towards Theo, for, even though he had the best head of hair of all Fairmount's male residents, including the expensively jacketed new resident she had this morning discovered in the wheelchair by the front office, Stella noticed that Theo seemed sad these days. His unhappiness was enough to break her heart, rather like the way Theo's much younger wife had broken Theo's heart by carrying on with her life in the great world outside, without him. It had become Stella's daily goal to make Theo smile.

In her search for Theo, she passed Thelma, who was making her way towards the dining room at a pace even slower than usual, pretending that her hip wasn't paining her.

"Let me help," Stella begged Thelma, as she had done every day this week.

"No help. Just tell me if I'm aimed right for breakfast."

"I think so. You know I get confused in the corridors." She joked, "The directionless leading the blind …"

"I'm not blind," Thelma said. "I have macular degeneration."

Thelma did indeed retain a wisp of peripheral vision, so Stella was careful to keep out of her view as she tailed Thelma safely to the dining room door, from whence she returned to questing for Theo. She rounded corner after corner without result until she found herself, Alice-like, back outside the Warden's office. The wheelchair fellow with the linen jacket was no longer there. No doubt a care worker had wheeled him off to settle him into his new room.

And here came Theo at last, striding around the next of Fairmount's many turnings. She walked up to meet him, and he stopped. He looked at her with such gravity and kindness that she wanted to hold onto him and never let go. She hid her feelings, smiled, and drew upon her teaching experience, which included thirty years of children telling her jokes. She said, *"Knock, knock."*

Theo nodded but didn't answer; along with a broken heart, Theo had tinnitus, and she tried never to take his silence as a personal affront. He inclined his head to her and hiked off at speed along the corridors, while Stella followed hard in his traces. She caught up with him in Corridor Park, where he stopped, and Stella worked to catch her breath.

The Greek Chorus scowled up at them both, for Iolanthe and Lucille were grumpy before their morning coffee, and Sally was downright green-pea jealous of Theo's friendship with Stella.

Stella repeated to Theo and the Greek Chorus, "Now, then, everybody. You know the drill. *Knock, knock.*"

Theo tipped his head towards her. "Sorry?"

His tinnitus must have been exceptionally bad today.

"*Knock, knock.*"

"No jokes, curse you," Lucille said. "I can't laugh on an empty stomach. When in the name of Julia Child is breakfast?"

Against the odds, Iolanthe came to Stella's rescue. "I will answer *knock, knock* with *who's there?* if it has anything to do with breakfast."

Stella said, "Ha! This joke will suit you perfectly."

Theo took a step towards a bend in the corridor, and she took hold of his arm. She would not allow him to walk off without having smiled.

Iolanthe and Stella chorused, "*Knock, knock.*" Sally glowered.

Theo asked, "Pardon?"

"Saints defend us and send food," Lucille muttered.

"*Knock, knock.*"

Theo said, "*Who's there?*"

Stella answered, "*Dozen.*"

"Er, *Dozen who?*"

Stella pictured the kindergarten student who had first told her his version of this particular joke. He'd run away, laughing, down the front steps of the school, kicking through the red and yellow maple leaves to the jungle gym where his friends hung upside down and chattered like monkeys. God in heaven, how she missed her school, her teaching friends, and above all the kids. Of course, that particular kindergartner would now be in his fifties.

"*Dozen who?*" Theo repeated.

Or his sixties. Could it be possible?

Iolanthe took hold of Stella's trouser pocket and shook it. *"Dozen who?"*

"Dozen anybody want something good to eat?"

Stella hurried away from the group towards the dining room, where Thelma was likely waiting for her. But before she turned the corner, she looked back, and thank all that was good in the world, Theo was smiling.

Throughout her life in the outside world, Stella had liked her breakfasts to be the same each day, and in this one aspect of Fairmount menu planning she was satisfied. Since the morning she had left home in her twentieth year, thus shuffling off the mortal pot of porridge her mother had served throughout Stella's childhood, she had by choice eaten toast with marmalade for breakfast. And, on the side, black tea. She got exactly that at Fairmount. True, there had been an issue with the marmalade supply chain a few weeks back, when the Greek Chorus had surrounded and captured every packet in the dining room for their own table. Since then, a small condiment skirmish had decided matters in Stella's favour, and recently a Nameless Dear care worker had forcibly united the two half-empty tables so that she, Thelma, and the Greek Chorus shared marmalade toast together at Stella's table, far from the window but close to the door.

The Greek Chorus did not like this table. They felt it was badly placed. Iolanthe and Lucille grumbled that they missed the light from the window, but they never looked at the window when they said it. They frowned at the table next to theirs, where the Rose Corridor residents sat. They were, every one, rumoured to be incontinent, as if that were anybody's business but their own.

And now their bottles of medications had gone missing. Stella thought back to the empty medicine bottles she had discovered in the locked room,[1] with Rose Corridor resident Wanda's name printed on it. Where were the pills that belonged in the bottles, and where were Dolores, Norma, Mildred, Florence, and Roberta of Rose Corridor's pills and bottles? Statistics argued that they couldn't all have misplaced them at the same time. One thing was certain, though: no matter who was responsible for the pills' disappearance, the Rose Corridor women were clearly victims of institutional bullying, and Stella made it a point to stop by their table each morning with a cheerful greeting.

This morning she made her usual stop to smile at the lot of them, conscious all the while of the Greek Chorus's scowls against her shoulder blades.

She asked Rose Corridor, "How are we all on this sunny morning?"

From the far side of the table, Dolores said, "We are sick of being in the doghouse, that's how we are."

Next to Dolores, Wanda said, "Mrs Warren wants us all to go to her office after breakfast."

Stella said, "It'll be all right."

The six women looked up: Dolores, Mildred, Wanda, Norma, Florence, and Roberta. Their teacups stood untouched before them, and their hands rested in their laps as if they had nowhere else to go.

It would not be all right. Not unless somebody made it all right. Dolores, Mildred, and Wanda were what Stella thought of as tough birds like herself, but it was asking a lot of them

---

[1] See *Stella Ryman and the Locked Room Mystery, Pulp Literature* Issue 23.

to protect a whole corridor of vulnerable women from Fairmount's Director.

She said, "It seems to me that Mrs Warren, our Director, is picking on you six."

"We think so too," Dolores said. "Even before the drugs started going missing, she acted out to get us."

"She told everybody that we're incontinent," Norma added.

Stella nearly said, *Ich bin incontinent.* She did say, "We are all incontinent."

"*We* certainly are not," Iolanthe said from the adjacent table.

"Be quiet," Thelma snapped. "It's a metaphor."

"It's not a metaphor," Stella said. "We are all incontinent. There's not a person in this dining room who hasn't peed when she laughs or leaked after a long morning in front of the TV. And that goes for Mrs Warren, too."

"It happened to me when I was eighteen." Mildred smiled palely. "On the West Boulevard, in front of a dry cleaner's."

"I peed myself when I was forty-seven," Lucille admitted. "I was in a crowded elevator and somebody said something funny."

The six women of Rose Corridor sat up a little straighter. Residents at the tables around them were listening with apparent interest. Stella didn't want to catch the attention of the care workers scattered here and there around the dining room, pushing residents close to the tables and settling paper napkins on laps, but she said what she wanted to say loud enough for the nearest tables to hear. "We mustn't let those in charge make us feel ashamed of ourselves."

"What does any of this matter?" Norma asked starkly. "Our lives are over, dear."

"*I'm* not dead yet," Thelma interjected.

Stella's blood seethed with the desire to climb up on the table and speak her mind out loud. *Listen to me, you residents of Fairmount: we here may have few contributions left to give this world, for we are like the famed lilies of the field, who do not toil anymore; but we have toiled. In fact, over the decades of our rich lives, we've given our share and even more. Therefore, the hours of our lives matter just as much as anyone's.*

Platters of toast were now being placed in the centre of each table, and care workers approached with tea and coffee in stainless-steel pots. Stella, bold words unspoken but stirring her spirit nonetheless, took her seat. She accepted a packet of marmalade when Lucille pointedly offered it.

Iolanthe raised her little finger and sipped tea from her mug. "Stella, you're a detective. Why don't you find out why the Warden bullies Rose Corridor?"

"Stella knows why. It's a law of nature." Thelma said. "Rose Corridor women don't do anything mean to anybody, so they get bullied."

Sally snorted, and Lucille shook her head. "The Warden bullies Stella, and Stella does plenty to deserve it."

"That's not bullying, dear," Iolanthe explained gently. "That's battling."

Stella laughed through her mouthful of toast. She had never liked Iolanthe much, but that remark raised within her a bushel of unexpected loving feelings.

Stella asked, "Isn't there a civilization somewhere where the elderly are esteemed?"

Iolanthe said dryly, "Yes, I saw it on a public-television documentary. The place is called Cloud Cuckoo Land."

Stella said, "Why must we be bossed and bullied here? Is it really the only way to run a care home?"

"Reliza doesn't bully," Thelma said. "Nor Cheryl, nor Ollie."

"They're the exceptions," Stella countered.

"Apparently, a place full of old people attracts pushy workers," Iolanthe said. "They must get satisfaction out of bossing their elders around."

"That's all very well," Stella said. "But bullying Rose Corridor is exceptionally disturbing behaviour by management."

"Look for the money," Thelma said.

"What money? There's no money," Iolanthe said.

"There's always money," Thelma replied.

"Huh. I can't see it," Lucille said. "What I see is that bossy board woman Audrey something, every time she swans into Fairmount. It's my belief she's watching us so she can pick off the weakest, kick us out of here, and fill our rooms with folks who don't need much help."

Stella thought of Ruby, naked in her chair.

"I wouldn't be surprised." Iolanthe sighed. "We'll have to pretend to be supple fifty-year-olds now. If we show any weakness, they'll ship us off to bed rest in public hospital wards."

Lucille said, "Be careful who sees you with that hip, Thelma."

"What hip?" Thelma scowled. "There's nothing wrong with my hip."

Cheryl, the care worker with the Mona Lisa smile, and her dodgy care worker ex-husband Riley, looked across at them from Rose Corridor's table, where Cheryl was touching a napkin to Roberta's long and buttery nose. She walked over to the table. "How is your hip, Ms Hu?"

"My hip is fine. My hip smells like a rose." Thelma pushed back her chair as if to get to her feet. "Watch me jump up and dance the bossa nova."

"That's wonderful. I worry about you, that's all." Cheryl moved off towards the tray of toast that Enid the cook was placing on the stainless-steel counter outside the kitchen.

"But your hip is giving you so much pain," Iolanthe said, and Sally nodded.

"There is nothing wrong with my hip." Thelma moved in her chair, and her grimace gave the lie to her words. "I am fine."

Thelma's hip was by nobody's measure fine. But Stella couldn't help worrying that for Thelma, a trip to hospital, especially for a hip operation, might be a one-way journey.

Stella shivered. She was unexpectedly overcome by the sensation of being herself on a one-way journey that would end too soon. She imagined herself at the rail of a big shabby boat, lightly crewed and steering straight over the edge of the world. *Here be dragons.* But at least on this, her final journey, they were serving toast with marmalade. She took a bite and washed it down with black tea.

Dr Terry rushed into the dining room and pulled Cheryl aside, speaking in low, hurried tones. The two stood not far from Stella's table, where she sat eating her last piece of marmalade toast slowly and with concentration, as if she were being careful of her teeth and not fully engaged as an amateur sleuth investigating the mysteries affecting Fairmount staff and residents. As if eating toast and looking out the window were all she had to do that morning. As if she were not straining to eavesdrop on Dr Terry's every hissed word.

"The Board is coming," he said. "Audrey wants to address the residents. Something about ticking boxes."

"What boxes?" Cheryl asked.

"I don't know. But heads up—they're on the way."

But that was where Dr Terry was wrong because, clearly visible through the glass in the dining room door, a small fast-stepping group of people was arriving. The door opened. The Board was not on its way; it was here.

The dining room door opened to admit a small group of confident, casually dressed men and women. At their heels, the ubiquitous new care worker, Riley, pushed an elderly man in a wheelchair into the room. The latter wore a linen jacket, and Stella recognized the fellow whose chair and lapel she'd straightened that morning while he slept. He was wide awake now, and, like everyone, far better looking than when he had been sleeping with his mouth open. So he was not, after all, a new resident; he was a member of the Board. He looked a few years older than Stella, perhaps Thelma's age, but he was clearly here to tour the facility and observe its residents, not to be toured and observed himself. Stella was about to formally dislike him as a quisling against elderly rights when he partly redeemed himself by jamming one wheel up against the door so that Riley had to squeeze himself on the far side of the wheelchair and wiggle the trapped wheel free. Residents chewed their toast and watched this bit of drama with evident interest.

Once the door was clear, the Warden bustled in after the small group of board members. She waved for residents' attention. "Let me introduce the Board. This is our chairperson, Mrs Audrey Frederick——"

Mrs Audrey Frederick interrupted the Director with cheerful callousness. "Perdita, I think that's my job, don't you? Thanks so much. And I want everyone to call me Audrey."

"Of course, Audrey." The Warden stepped back.

"For those of you who don't remember your board members, I'm Audrey, and this is my father, Vaughn. You'll all know the sports radio host Kenny, and Rhonda and Todd, both leaders in the world of real estate."

The members of the Board waved like stars and said good morning. Stella studied Audrey, to see whether this middle-aged, suit-clad chairperson might be worth liking, since she'd so firmly put the Warden in her place. But Audrey had a look in her eye and a jut to her chin that was familiar to Stella from her days in the educational system, when folks with similar expressions whipped parent-teacher evenings into submission with lashing resolutions. Stella decided she had no more love for this bully than she had for the Warden.

Audrey continued, "It's lovely to see all of you here, enjoying the tasty breakfast your director has planned and your cooks have carried out here for you on spotless trays. I'll bet not one of you misses your cruise ship days when mealtimes roll around . . ."

Stella sat back to evaluate the board members as a group. They were all tricked out in sporty attire with their well-shod feet planted hardily on Fairmount Manor flooring; in Vaughn's case, his gleaming boots were set wide upon his wheelchair footrests. Stella reminded herself that, Vaughn aside, these men and women with their sturdy poses of command were only a few decades younger than the Fairmount residents. She imagined the Board in thirty years, dressed in fleece leisure suits, the knees of their track pants sagging and their pockets full of lint. Why should simple chronology give these people so much power? They could, with a word and a signature, allow Stella and her associates more food or less; better care or worse; improved facilities or the status quo.

Audrey continued, "I'm glad to see you all well and happy, enjoying visitors, trips to the mall, and activities in the activities hall. I think I'd better join you there today, for the sake of my own figure." She laughed. Her figure was fine.

Stella judged that Audrey was one of those speakers who made it her business to make eye contact with every person in the room, from Fairmount's director — shifting from one foot to the other — to each care worker, and finishing up with every resident at every table. When it was Stella's turn for the chairperson's gaze to meet hers, she likened it to a steely grip upon her upper arm. On the positive side, she got no feeling from Audrey's gaze that she was being pictured in her underwear.

"… And let's not forget to thank your staff, the care workers we call angels among us, who do the heavy lifting so that you can enjoy your sunny days and busy, activity-filled lives …" Audrey's attention moved to Rose Corridor's table, where Dolores, Norma, Mildred, Wanda, Florence, and Roberta wilted under her gaze. Audrey's focus lingered upon them as she spoke, as if she had heard talk about Rose Corridor and had opinions about the residents at that table. The contrast between the gleaming Audrey and the limp-haired, sad-eyed, undermedicated women of Rose Corridor gave Stella a flash of unmixed loathing for the person or persons who had placed Rose Corridor's women in this position. Someone had stolen their medications and left them to fall without a pharmaceutical net into last place in competence among the residents. Had Riley stolen their medicine? She contemplated him as he stood behind Vaughn's wheelchair. Was that a new shirt he wore beneath his tidy care worker's zip smock? She attempted deduction from this admittedly limited data.

1. His shirt collar was visible, open at his neck, and that might mean a missing button. If so, an old shirt on a vain young man might indicate a lack of disposable income, and thus innocence of drug dealing.
2. But equally, the open neck might just be the fashion or, if not, then possibly a further indication of his lackadaisical attitude, not only to his work here at Fairmount but to his family obligations to Cheryl and their children. But an open shirt collar did not mean he had stolen Rose Corridor's drugs.

Stella frowned. She wasn't convinced that drug dealing would or even could occur in a place like Fairmount Manor Care Home. There was no back alley here, no concrete graffitied stairwell as seen on television. More importantly, stealing elderly women's meds was unlikely to bring in a cocaine dealer's income. And, most importantly, even if Riley did steal the meds, theft was not what most threatened Rose Corridor. Doctor Terry could get the women another prescription, and Riley could get himself fired, but Rose Corridor would still be in danger of being separated and sent away from the only friends and the only home they knew. And Stella was confident that right here before her was that great threat to life and happiness: the Board of Directors.

And they were not a distant threat, either, for Stella observed Audrey's gaze return frequently to Dolores, Mildred, Wanda, Norma, Florence, and Roberta, and she deduced that something perilous loomed for them all.

Audrey gave the Rose Corridor table a final, piercing look and then beamed at the residents at large. "Together with your Board, you'll also want to thank those who helped you find your way to Fairmount: your loved ones who cared enough to send you where you'll get the unique blend of care and independence that Fairmount offers. We have today sent each of your families a letter, laying out emerging and developing parameters of care as they will unfold here over the coming months."

Stella sat up and listened well. Unfold how?

Audrey's smile widened with the scope of her words. "Independence and respect for all our residents remain paramount for us members of the Board, and we plan to dedicate Fairmount, this homeplace, to that end. That is why we will be keeping close records, now, of residents who can continue to enjoy Fairmount's free and breezy style of living, and those who would benefit from a move to another facility with a more focussed, hands-on approach. But if you don't need help toileting, if you can get yourself up and ready for the day on your own, if you can walk unaided — walkers are fine, of course — if you know the day of the week and enjoy and recognize your visitors when they arrive to spend precious moments with you, you can be sure that every day at Fairmount will be a great day for you. Thank you."

Stella studied each board member with loathing. These people stood before their elders, chests out, hands in the pockets of expensive clothing that Fairmount residents were not likely to possess again in this lifetime. They cast condescending looks on Rose Corridor's table and maybe even gloried in their power to send residents to an uncertain future in a palliative hospital. For that was what Audrey's speech came down to. It was a hammer poised over every white and bald head.

Many leave Fairmount for hospital, but few return.

The five ambulant board members gave a final wave and made their way around Vaughn's wheelchair and into the corridor, while Vaughn waited. Once the rest of the Board was through, Riley attempted to manoeuvre Vaughn's wheelchair through the door, but the older man held up a hand. Riley halted and held the door open with his foot as Dolores and Norma helped their less agile Rose Corridor neighbours — Wanda, Florence, and Roberta — out of the dining room. When the way was clear, Riley pushed Vaughn's chair through after them.

At their own table, the Greek Chorus set to dusting toast crumbs off their breasts and began to get to their feet. Thelma kept a hand on Stella's arm while care workers cleared the tables, and when they were too far off to overhear her, she hissed, "Let's get me to my chair before that Audrey woman sees my limp and has me embalmed where I stand."

Lucille said, "Better than cremated."

Iolanthe said, "I want to be cremated. But not yet, obviously."

Lucille said, "I want to ripen and fall from the branch."

Sally nodded.

Stella held open the dining room door for the Greek Chorus to pass through, and then jammed the door open with a chair. She helped Thelma to her feet and out the door, doing her best to shield Thelma's limp from view of the care workers still bussing the dining room. Once outside in the corridor, she found the coast was still not clear, for here were the Rose Corridor women, Theo Longbourne, Vaughn in his wheelchair, and Riley.

Stella looped her arm through Thelma's. Thelma sagged against her.

"Hold on," Stella said. "Try to stand up straight."

"Tell that to Mr Gravity."

Stella held Thelma upright and did her best to make it look easy while she evaluated the situation. To her right, down the corridor towards the office, the women of Rose Corridor clustered outside a washroom door, whispering together and shooting glances at Stella and Thelma. They were no threat to Thelma, of course; they had enough to worry about with their own troubles, including missing medications. Theo Longbourne strode around them towards the office, but Theo was a friend, and furthermore spoke so infrequently it was hard to imagine him inadvertently betraying Thelma and her sore hip to the authorities.

The two men directly in front of Stella and Thelma were the stumbling blocks. Vaughn, with his back to them, blocked their way with his wheelchair, while Riley, also turned away, was busy fiddling with his foot at the chair's brake. He was making quite a business of it, rattling the mechanism with the toe of his shoe (well-worn canvas slip-on, Stella noted, with the mark of his toenail clearly showing through the fabric) and then bending over to poke at the brake with his fist.

Vaughn, apparently unaware that Stella and Thelma had emerged from the dining room, spoke. With a nod towards the women of Rose Corridor, he asked Riley, "Don't you find it extraordinary that, all things being equal in age and infirmity" — Vaughn patted the arm of the wheelchair — "I am on the Board and those ladies over there are not?"

Riley straightened. "Not at all, sir."

"That was a very quick answer."

"Well, sir, when you think about it, you've taken care of yourself all these years, and you've worked hard to earn money so that you can stay in your own home. You can pay for your own home care. Everybody here could have done the same, including all those Rose Corridor ladies."

Stella felt Thelma's grip tighten on her arm. Forty years of teaching school exchanged a look of disbelief with sixty years of twelve-hour days keeping a neighbourhood corner store.

Riley smiled down at Vaughn, man to man. "Life is what we make it, am I right?"

Vaughn nodded. "You'd better go, young man."

"Yes, sir? Can I get you something?"

"Well, you can. After that nasty little speech, you can get going. In fact, you have ten seconds to get out of my sight before I fire you."

Riley started, stared, and walked quickly away with a look over his shoulder at Vaughn. The latter reached down, released his brake with the ease of much practice, and spun his chair around to face Stella and Thelma.

Beyond Vaughn's wheelchair stretched one of Fairmount's winding corridors, and at a certain point in its vagaries was the safe haven of Corridor Park. There Iolanthe and the Greek Chorus stitched pillowcases without hope of Ulysses's return, and there Thelma would be free to sit in her chair with her sore hip undiscovered by the authorities. Stella tucked Thelma's small hand around her elbow and pulled her closer. She frowned at Vaughn, willing him to move on so that she could help Thelma to safety. Why didn't he turn his wheelchair? Why did he stare at her so?

Vaughn said, "Thank you."

Stella answered, "You're welcome. But I'm not sure what for."

"You helped me this morning when I dozed off and missed the meeting of the Board. In my wheelchair predicament, you spared me some embarrassment."

"Embarrassment!" Thelma snorted. "That's an expensive treat around Fairmount."

Stella said, "It was a pleasure." She thought it better not to mention that she'd leaped to the conclusion that Vaughn was a fellow resident. He might be about Stella's age, but he was clearly a man of power who could, with a word, accomplish things of which Stella herself could only dream, like firing Riley and exiting through Fairmount's front door whenever he liked. He was a man, simply put, whom Stella couldn't trust. And she therefore couldn't let him spot Thelma's infirmity. She placed herself firmly between Vaughn and Thelma and began to move slowly past him along the corridor.

Thelma took seven steps and then stopped. While she rested, Stella cocked an eye over her shoulder to see whether Vaughn had rolled his wheelchair away, perhaps towards the little group of Rose Corridor women by the washroom. His wheelchair was one of those quiet, titanium models that you could almost play basketball from. It was not motorized, and it moved so noiselessly that she couldn't simply listen to learn where Vaughn was. She had to look.

He hadn't moved an inch. In fact, he'd turned his wheelchair again, and the bloody man was staring after her and Thelma. She positioned herself still more carefully to hide Thelma's limp, gave him what she hoped was a friendly, valedictory smile, and the two made their way a little farther along the path to Corridor Park. She was congratulating herself on their progress when she heard some among the Rose Corridor women sniffing and others offering words of comfort and dismay. Stella longed to stop, to see whether she could help out or at least reassure the beleaguered six that they had at least one champion. And she would. But she had to first get Thelma safely to her chair. It occurred to her that if Vaughn was really the gentleman he seemed to be, he might turn his attention to helping the weeping Rose Corridor residents.

She moved Thelma two more steps towards Corridor Park, and then Vaughn in his wheelchair approached from behind, passed them, and stopped in front of them, effectively barring their passage.

"I can't help noticing," Vaughn said, "that one of you is having trouble walking."

"Pot," Thelma said. "Kettle."

Stella nudged Thelma to be silent. To Vaughn she explained, "It's just a little crick in her leg. She'll be better if she can get to her chair to rest it."

"Right." Vaughn studied the two of them. "It sounds unlikely, though. I can't help worrying, especially because of my position on the Board."

"Well, if I'm such a problem, why don't you send me off to hospital?" Thelma asked with poisonous sweetness. "I'll never come back, and then you won't have to worry about me any more at all."

Vaughn blinked. He studied Thelma's face, and then Stella's.

Clearly, this exchange was unsalvageable, and Stella moved Thelma a little more quickly past Vaughn and along the corridor. If she and Thelma could manage to sink anonymously back into the greater community of Fairmount residents, they might well be overlooked. Or even forgotten, for if the gods of Olympus had granted one supernatural power to otherwise powerless people, it was invisibility.

But Vaughn in his wheelchair passed them again and turned the back of his chair to them. "Hop on," he said.

Stella remembered sitting on Theo's lap[2] in his short time in a wheelchair not long ago. It had been rather fun. Something

---

[2] See *Stella Ryman and the Fairmount Manor Mysteries*.

to make her feel special after what, she recalled, was a very challenging day.

But Thelma shot Vaughn's wheelchair a black look. "You've got a nerve. Around here, if you ride on somebody's wheelchair with them, you have to marry them."

Vaughn snorted. "Ride on the back then. See, there's a little bar there for your toes. My grandkids ride on it all the time. Climb on, and tell me where I can drop you."

Stella tucked Thelma's cane under her arm and helped her onto the back of the chair. The rear bar of the wheelchair was narrow, and she had to help Thelma hold on. Stella kept her own feet, in their lace-up shoes, firmly on the floor while she struggled along, impelling the chair and its two occupants forward as best she could while Vaughn worked his push rims and Thelma directed the way to Corridor Park. The sound of the three of them, all over eighty and panting like a Victorian train engine, echoed from walls and ceiling.

A ride that involved three active people on four wheels was rather a committee effort. However, unlike many committee efforts of Stella's long experience in the public school system, it succeeded beautifully. The heavily-laden wheelchair, propelled by Vaughn's machine-like arm movements, Stella's steady pressure from behind, and Thelma's strength of personality, shivered the three of them into Corridor Park.

The Greek Chorus looked up from their seats near Stella and Thelma's empty chairs. Iolanthe, Lucille, and Sally registered surprise by throwing their needlework down on their laps. On their far side, Theo halted mid-stride in his customary morning ramble. All four gaped as Vaughn's wheelchair decanted Thelma into her own seat. Stella tucked Thelma's cane into her hands so that the rubber-tipped end rested between her red silk slippers.

"I knew it." Lucille shook her head. "I knew that if I sat here in this corridor long enough, a bus would come along."

Vaughn smiled. "Hold very tight, please, and have your fares ready."

At this quip the Greek Chorus moved happily in their chairs.

Stella regarded Vaughn with more warmth than she had ever expected to feel for a member of the Board. In his expensive suit and still more expensive wheelchair, he looked rather handsome for a man with quite a bit of hair in his ears. Stella had not in her long life interacted often with powerful, wealthy people. Certainly she had never dated anybody more aristocratic than an all-business civil engineer in her first year of Normal School, before she'd started her teaching career. Now, gazing with appreciation at this prince of wealth and influence in his pricey wheelchair, she felt power's attraction. When she was young, it had been acceptable for a girl to dream that a prince might rescue a maiden. She imagined the swoop of Vaughn's limousine up to Fairmount's door, how he would help Thelma and Stella into its lush interior; she could almost feel the cold flute of bubbly wine he would hand to her and Thelma while his long black vehicle drove them off to . . .

Where?

Here Stella's romantic imagination abandoned her. She laughed silently at girlish limousine imaginings, and, still smiling, looked past Vaughn to meet Theo's gaze. He smiled back.

And that was two smiles from Theo today. With Theo sorted and Thelma settled, Stella moved towards her own chair under the skylight. She brushed away a couple of drops of condensation that had fallen onto its seat from the skylight's frame and was about to sit down when Vaughn turned his wheelchair to face her.

"I could use a guide to the front door," he said. "Will you show me how to get there?"

"I'd be embarrassed to try. Sorry, my sense of direction is a bust," Stella explained.

"You might as well ask Alice to show you around Wonderland," Iolanthe offered. "The farther Stella travels towards the front door, the farther away it moves."

Lucille cackled, and Sally the Nodder nodded.

"We'll find our way," Vaughn assured them.

Stella had, over the past couple of months, trained herself not to say *it's your funeral* to anybody at Fairmount. Furthermore, arguing politely with Vaughn seemed like a waste of her time left on earth.

Stella fell into step with Vaughn in his wheelchair. She glanced down at him and reflected that she didn't have far to look because, even when seated, he was a tall man—nearly as tall, she judged, as Theo. Stella discovered that walking side by side with Fairmount Manor's most senior, or rather oldest, board member was a strangely convivial experience. He rolled; she strolled. And for a few moments they walked in the silence that often settles happily on old friends. She wondered whether he felt equally amicable towards her, or whether it was an ambience he generated around everybody he met, a sort of aura that would have contributed to his prestige and success in the outside world over the years of his life. She felt relaxed and positive in Vaughn's company. In fact, she felt young in his company, for she was at present reminded of her years in high school, particularly of unhurried walks between classes on warm afternoons. As she had done back at school, she placed the flat of her palm against the walls and dragged it along the cool surface, wondering why doing something useless just because one had done it long ago was so very satisfying.

Vaughn broke the silence. "I'm worried about your friend Thelma. She's obviously in pain."

"She thinks her hip will heal on its own," Stella said. "It has before. She wants to give it some time."

"I keep thinking, shouldn't we get a doctor to look at it?"

"X-rays?" Stella frowned. "Possibly an operation?"

"Well, yes. That is, after all, how modern medicine can help."

"You'd think so, wouldn't you? Unless you lived here at Fairmount."

"I don't understand."

"Exactly." Stella smiled tightly.

Vaughn frowned. He set his brake and gazed down at the corridor floor. Stella recognized this as the sort of power pause a certain school principal of her acquaintance employed: a moment of silence that worked to strengthen his point of view without raising hackles or voices. Often staff members or parents, overcome by the power pause, would begin babbling requests or excuses, but Stella was an old hand with the strategy. Since Vaughn was staring at the floor, Stella gazed up at the ceiling and, as had been her practice in staff meetings when the principal pulled such stunts, she began to count silently to herself.

She had reached twenty-three when Vaughn spoke.

"Please explain why you won't try to get Thelma to proper care."

Stella recited, "*Those who leave Fairmount seldom return.*"

Vaughn blinked. "Is that true?"

"It's a tenet around here. Therefore, it doesn't matter whether it's true. They ..." She corrected herself. "I mean, we at Fairmount believe it, and believing it makes it true enough to frighten us sparrows off the power lines."

"So, what if we absolutely need to send a Fairmount resident to hospital, for example for a heart attack or stroke? Or if they ask to go? You say we should keep them here?"

"Certainly not. You do have to send them to hospital. You must."

"But?"

"But they — *we* — often don't return. Unless it's to Palliative, upstairs. That means ..."

"I know what palliative means."

Did he? Stella doubted he knew Fairmount's palliative floor the way she knew it, or as Theo did, as a place from which they both at different moments[3] had narrowly escaped oblivion. For Thelma, a palliative care ward was a mortal peril she had yet to face.

Stella said, "Well, given that we all feel that those who leave Fairmount seldom return, you might make an effort to imagine why Thelma is being stubborn about wanting to deal with her hip on her own."

"Yes." Vaughn's lips tightened. "You must think we're monsters."

Stella said, "Monsters might be going a bit far. I don't think you board members want to bite us with your sharp teeth."

"Of course not."

"But you might accidentally trample us with your big unthinking feet."

Stella had hoped to make Vaughn laugh — Theo would certainly have laughed at the thought of board members in shiny

---

[3] See *Stella Ryman and the Fairmount Manor Mysteries*.

suits stomping like shiny-shoed Godzillas along Fairmount's corridors. But when she met Vaughn's gaze, she was startled to see a real warmth there. Not the sense of humour that Theo's watery blue eyes communicated, but something almost as nice. It was the look of a man who liked and respected her. Increasingly over the decades, and thanks to social evolution, Stella had met men who spoke to her in that respectful manner. She wondered whether, if she'd met Vaughn fifty or sixty years ago, he would have treated her with the same high regard, or if he'd learned to appreciate women as equals along the way. There was a third possibility, however, because having a hardline daughter like Audrey might well have forced him into an egalitarian outlook. She thought a little more kindly of Audrey and gestured towards the end of the corridor.

"So be it. Let's carry on." Vaughn flipped off his wheelchair brake. "But I reserve the right to check back on Thelma in a week or two."

"I'll check on her," Stella said briskly. She began walking, and he joined her, but this time Stella set the pace for both of them. She knew perfectly well that her sense of direction hadn't improved any in the last ten minutes, but she was not going to show Vaughn the great and powerful exactly how disoriented she could become.

She added, "I'll make myself responsible for Thelma's health."

Vaughn sighed and spoke words that gave away the truth of his generational attitude to women. "You're the kind of gal who gets her way."

"Am I?" She remembered a vice-principal who had said the same thing to her, and how she had replied. She answered Vaughn now as she'd answered her administrator then. "Or am I a person who gets her way?"

Vaughn laughed. "Sorry. *Person.* Fellows our age are guilty of enough misogyny. I'll try not to add to it."

"Oh, you're not doing so badly, believe me. Between ageist visitors, a heartless administration, and racist old fools everywhere at Fairmount, I'm becoming quite tough-skinned."

Vaughn frowned, and they rolled several steps in silence.

At last, in a soft voice that made him sound much younger than was, he said, "This place must be different from what you yourself are used to. What did you do before you retired?"

"Taught school." The phrase was inadequate to communicate the decades of laughter, worry, intellectual challenges, small sacrifices, and big joys her career in the school system had brought her. The years of her happy employment stretched out in memory as long as Fairmount's corridors, but straight rather than winding, so that she could see every classroom in her school: the seating arrangements, the art cupboards and classroom sinks, her library shelves neatly rowed with fiction and non-fiction volumes, and all her thousands of students, bright faced still in her recollection. She felt as if, should she try, she would remember each of their names, the ring of their voices, and the stamp of their shoes as they tore past her door out to recess. "I taught in an elementary school. All subjects, and I administered the library."

"Good for you," Vaughn said. "I haven't formally retired, but except for the Board, I haven't done a lick of what my daughter calls 'lawyer work' for seven and a half years, come June."

"Not that you're counting," Stella said.

"How long since your last day of work?"

"Seventeen years," Stella said. "They made me go at sixty-five, of course. I understand the rules have changed."

"Rules, maybe. Attitudes, no. How long have you been here?"

A thousand years. "A few months," Stella told him.

"I can't help thinking, *Here but for the grace of god.* I hope that's not offensive."

"Of course it is," Stella said. "But as I said, you'll have to work pretty hard to be offensive enough to get under my skin in this place."

"I don't think I'd like living here."

"Then don't."

"I won't. I don't like the idea of you living here either."

"Don't worry your head." Even to herself Stella sounded a bit fresh and flirty, but why not? "I'm all right."

"Are you?" Vaughn said. "You're still sharp. Why aren't you bored to death?"

Stella couldn't resist. "I'm a member of the bored, and you're a member of the Board."

"See? Still sharp. I wish there was something I could do to make things better for you."

"I have a roof over my head and food on my plate. Family if I want it, just like you."

"Not like me. I order my carers around like dogs."

Stella remembered his treatment of Riley and smiled. "I would never do that to Ollie and Cheryl. And Reliza wouldn't last a day."

"Don't change the subject. You live in a building that smells like urine and cleaning fluid. Isn't there anything I can do for you?"

"You can go to the board meetings. Vote for better funds for the cooks and more care workers. You know the drill. You must have dealt with union demands in your time."

"Sure, that's ongoing here." Vaughn shook his head. "I mean you, Mrs Stella Ryman. What do you need? You personally?"

Stella stopped at his side. She looked down at the toes of her good lace-up shoes, the ones she'd inherited from a dead woman, lined up evenly with the toes of Vaughn's gleaming boots. Were they Church's? Ingeldew's? Italy's best leather product? Her own lace-up shoes were the one thing she'd needed before she got them. Now, what was her great wish? A handbag. She missed the feel of her handbag on her arm.

"Freedom," she said. "That's what I want."

"Freedom." Vaughn tapped the padded arms of his wheelchair with the tips of his index fingers. "That's a rather loose term."

"And I'm sure it's different for you and me."

"Keep talking. What's freedom for you, Stella?"

"I suppose it's the power to leave Fairmount and walk outside, along the sidewalk, and into a corner store to purchase six cold beers for me and my friends and a bag of Hawkins Cheezies. To wear my own good clothes, linen and cashmere, and then return with my purchases to my own home. Can you give me that, I wonder?"

Vaughn didn't answer.

They passed the office where the secretary's desk used to stand. Stella looked back at the Warden's office door. Nearby was the spot where she had first seen Vaughn, bumped up against the wall and left alone with his wheelchair askew, an old man left to his slumbers while the younger members of the Board discussed issues vital to the administration of Fairmount Manor.

Vaughn rolled his wheelchair along with one arm while he fumbled in the pocket of his jacket and then contorted his torso to dig into his trouser pocket. He twisted to reach deeper.

Stella was so fascinated with his inexplicable movements that she almost missed their arrival at the front door, where the nurse's station stood empty.

"Here we are," Vaughn said.

Stella thought at first he meant *here we are at the door.* But he was holding out a fist full of something. She took it from him in her two hands and looked down to see whether it really was what it felt like.

"Freedom." Vaughn shrugged. "Power."

Stella's hands were so packed with paper money that it was all she could do to hold onto it before it scattered about Fairmount's foyer like autumn leaves across a school playground. Her mother's voice in her head said she ought not to accept such a gift from a man. The Warden's voice twitted her that she would never have anything on which to spend this money. She ignored them both and thanked him.

"No problem. Flowers in my garden," Vaughn said circumspectly. "Soup in my cupboard. Money in my bank."

Stella wasn't sure what he meant by these eccentric remarks and was even less certain that she wanted to ask. She gazed down at the paper money in her hands. The thick wad appeared to be made up primarily of twenties and hundreds. *Hundreds.*

Vaughn pressed the buttons on the keypad at the front door to exit. She decided that if his fingers trembled, or if he got the keypad numbers wrong, she would stop him and return his gift.

But his fingers were steady, just as steady as Theo's when he pressed those same buttons. Also like Theo—and unlike Stella herself—Vaughn got the numbers right the first time. Stella stepped forward, her hands still full of hundreds and twenties, and held the door open for him with her elbow. Vaughn nodded his thanks, but he was already looking ahead along Fairmount's entry path to the large grey SUV waiting there. He rolled his wheelchair through the door and onto the path.

Stella stood and stared after him. She gripped the wad of cash between her hands and wondered where she might safely conceal it. For nobody had to tell her that she would not be permitted to keep cash in large denominations. The saying *you can't take it with you* applied to entering a care home the same way it applied to death. Furthermore, the Warden's imagined sneer would be accurate, for there was not a darned thing she could buy with all this money at Fairmount. Still, the fact that she had it felt like a small but toothsome victory. She divided the bills into two thick wads and shoved them into her fleece trouser pockets.

Job done, and still holding open the foyer door, she breathed in the outside air, rich with the odour of Fairmount's laurel hedges. Their leaves were nearly yellow where the sun touched them, such a bright and heart-lifting hue that she was tempted to follow Vaughn outside and then stroll away down the sidewalk to even a short-lived freedom. The chances of real escape were few, and the prospect of capture and ignominious return a daunting one. Still, might it not be worth risking humiliation to step out into a world of clear May skies, budding roses, and the green tips of new conifer growth? She might have gone, too, swift as lines from *Poetry of Departures*—with a wink at Philip Larkin in poet's heaven—if she'd been alone. However, she wasn't alone. The shuffle of slip-on shoes creeping up behind heralded the arrival of several Fairmount residents. Perhaps they could all escape together? She turned and recognized the women of Rose Corridor bearing down upon her at the open door. Rose Corridor residents, outside? Much as it pained her to think like the

Warden and the Board, she worried that a car might hit one of them. Stella stepped away from the foyer door, and it closed with the shushing noise that Stella hated. It sounded as if the building were telling her, *Shh, you're all safe at Fairmount, so you've no reason to complain. After all, you have everything I want you to have.* And the click of the lock.

The six women of Rose Corridor crowded into Fairmount's foyer. Dolores, Mildred, Wanda, Norma, Florence, and Roberta gathered around Stella. Together they stared out the front windows at Fairmount's walkway. They had a perfect view of Vaughn being helped out of his wheelchair by his driver and into the back seat of the SUV. Stella took a step back to let Florence and Roberta, always the shyest of these women, get an excellent gander. The group stood close to one another, close as six fairytale sisters, and she remembered with a pang that she was meant to be solving the mystery of their missing medications.

Although, taking collective stock of the Rose Corridor residents, she observed with some surprise that they looked far more cheerful than they had at breakfast. More alert. Their colours were higher, and they chatted quietly among themselves about the sunny day and what might be for lunch (the consensus was packet chicken noodle soup). What had brought on such a change in their demeanour? There had not been time for replacement medications to arrive.

The driver folded Vaughn's wheelchair and set it inside the rear door of the SUV. He tugged shut the back hatch and climbed into the driver's seat, and the car pulled away.

Stella turned to the Rose Corridor women. "I'm sorry I've been so slow to discover what thief took your medications."

"I can tell you." Norma pointed at the departing car and stated, "*He did.* The man in the wheelchair."

A moment's silence followed Norma's pronouncement. All eyes turned from the windows and fixed upon Stella.

With deliberate calm, Stella asked, "Are you telling me that Vaughn, a board member, took your meds?"

"He did." Dolores frowned. "Did he? Are we sure?"

"Oh, yes," Mildred agreed. She nudged Wanda and Roberta on either side. They nodded.

Florence said, "What? Yes?"

Norma nodded. "He said he'd bring our pills back, but he never did."

Stella gazed at each of the Rose Corridor women, friends to the end. Stella was grateful to have Thelma as a girlfriend, and she knew the Greek Chorus members were as happy in each other's company as three snappish witches could be. Still, she wondered how it would be to be *six* chums who could count on each other day and night. Stella had always felt sorry for these Rose Corridor residents. These women were always the slowest to begin and finish meals, holding up the advent of cups of tea and coffee while they nibbled crusts and spilled soup from their spoons back into their bowls. They were the butt of all incontinence rumours and, as of this morning, the evident targets of the Board's crackdown on unreliable residents. But now, seeing these women's united front, she envied them.

"Vaughn took the meds, you say?"

"Do you believe us?" Norma asked anxiously.

"It would be useful to have proof," Stella explained. She had for evidence only the testimony of the women of Rose Corridor.

Stella read in their eager gazes a heart-tugging certainty of her fairness, regard, and consideration of their words. She wished she were actually an investigating police officer so that she might respectfully thank them and call in Vaughn for questioning. But she knew something that a police officer might not know: that Vaughn had everything—had so much of everything, in fact, that he was giving it away: witness the money he'd given Stella, now bulging the pockets of her fleece suit. He didn't need their medications, because he could buy whatever he needed.

But if she were completely, even robotically, objective, she had to admit that when Vaughn gave her all that money—thrust it, unasked, into her hands—he'd demonstrated such an inappropriate generosity of spirit that she was not entirely certain he was as *compos mentis* as he appeared to be. Though he wasn't feeding yesterday's tuna fish to a secret cat, of course. Yet.

Still, her deductive instincts told her Vaughn would not have stolen Rose Corridor's medications. (The phrase *deductive instincts* was arguably an oxymoron, like *genuine Naugahyde*, but she had long ago learned in her teaching career that, with practice, one gained intuition for any challenging work.) Therefore, if

1. Vaughn were indeed innocent, as she believed, then it followed
2. that these apparently fragile and put-upon women from Rose Corridor were the classic detective's challenge, the test of any accomplished sleuth: lying witnesses.

Stella would have to break them somehow, and she had to do it without browbeating them or making anybody cry.

"My dears," she began, "you seem very well. Much better than I feel, in fact."

Norma blinked. "Oh, that's nice of you to say."

Stella added, "I feel like an old rubber band. Or a holey sock."

Wanda rolled her eyes in agreement. "I used to get that feeling all the time."

Florence ventured, "I feel just like that when I've not had my yellow pills."

"Yellow pills, yes. You should try them, Stella," Wanda said.

Dolores suggested, "You might ask Dr Terry if you can take them."

"The red pills are the real firecrackers, though," Norma added.

Wanda said, "Maybe. I must say, though, I can't even get out of bed without my yellow pills."

Stella asked, "Are they round or oblong?"

Wanda dug in her pocket and brought out a screwed-up bit of tissue. "Look, they're round."

Wanda pulled at the tissue and revealed several yellow pills.

Stella nodded thoughtfully. "Is that the best one? The yellow one?"

Now Dolores dipped into her pockets. "Oh, no, that's for blood. Inflammation's the best one, the red one, but you have to build up to it for a few days."

Norma nodded. "Oh, yes, that's true. Once you start you can't stop, or you have to build up again."

Here was another thing a real police detective might not be aware of: every Fairmount resident was proud of his or her medications, a little the way Stella remembered being proud of her high school back in the day.

Now all six of the Rose Corridor women were digging in their pockets.

"Now, the orange pills …"

"Yes, still, you know, the yellow …"

How Stella longed for the traditional unmasking. How she wished she could produce an *aha!* And wave it about like a flag. *J'accuse, mes amies de Rose Corridor.* You stole those medications from yourselves and kept them, and are now waiting on the new batch from Dr Terry.

She watched them, feeling more love for these women now than she had even before she knew they'd lied and accused an innocent man in a wheelchair.

Mildred was saying, "Take the blue ones at bedtime, on an empty stomach, no matter what the instructions say."

"Oh, the instructions!" Dolores laughed indulgently. "I *take* those with a pinch of salt."

"Still, you must be careful. You don't want to take more than your dose, or you'll run out."

Now the Rose Corridor women spoke together, one overtop the other.

"You don't want to run out."

"Keep some of your medications aside."

"Riley lost ours. Then he found them, so we got extra."

Aha. Stella asked, "Riley lost your medications?" *Or said he did.*

"And then he talked about, you know …" Wanda coloured.

Mildred was made of stronger stuff. "Incontinence."

"And then we weren't, because we hardly ever are."

"Except a few times for …" There was a pause, and everybody looked at everybody else, except Florence and Roberta. "But none of us told."

"And then Riley gave the pills back."

"Why?" But Stella knew why. She had witnessed Riley with the bouquet of flowers he'd given her, to soften her, and then, imagining she would forget, had given the same flowers to Reliza, to ease his way with her as well. It was the sort of thing he would do — withhold Rose Corridor's medications unless they stayed continent or cleaned up after themselves. To make morning chores easier for him.

"So we kept the pills. In case he did it again," Mildred said.

"We kept them all. I don't think he noticed, really."

Stella said, "Riley is an incompetent fellow."

"Oh, he's like all the care workers. They lose everything."

"Or the doctor, you know he's in love."

"With that Reliza."

"Nobody can get things right when they're in love."

Stella said, "I'll write the pill colours down so I remember."

Nodding and helping one another as they moved, the women of Rose Corridor shuffled away from Stella, past the empty nurse's window, and along the corridor.

She called after them, "Thank you very much indeed. Where are you off to now?"

They didn't answer. Nor could she blame them for their non-response, for where was there to go? The activities hall, their own corridor, and soon enough the dining room for packet chicken noodle soup and, eventually, a warmish cup of tea.

You had to hand it to Rose Corridor for nerve and cool. Because Riley threatened to withhold their medications, the women had stolen their own meds, lied about their disappearance, and hoarded more.

Stella grimaced. She had solved a mystery, and what was her reward? Was it, as for Hammett's amateur sleuths Nick and Nora Charles, a flute of cold champagne and dinner on the town? No. Not even a cold beer and Cheezies with her friends. Her reward was lukewarm tea. Eventually.

Stella decided that as her prize for solving the mystery of Rose Corridor's stolen medications, she should have a nice mug of properly hot tea. And she should have it now. Or as close to now as a raid on the care worker's staff room could be. She smoothed the bulges in her trouser pockets and decided that once she had stolen a nice mug of tea from the staff room, she would take it with her into the storage room, under the shelter of the art table with its green plastic tablecloth. She would enjoy her solitude, count the cash Vaughn had given her, and see how unnecessarily rich she had become.

Perhaps Mad Cassandra Browning would find her there, as she had done once before. Company, even the company of a woman who had in all probability died years ago, would be acceptable. Better than acceptable, really, for although Mad Cassandra was unlikely to be much help counting money, she would certainly enliven the morning. She would probably toss hundred-dollar bills around the storage cupboard and spill the tea. Stella laughed aloud at the thought. She might be just a bird in a Fairmount cage, but some of the company here was not bad. Not bad at all.

Stella turned a corner that she was certain would lead into Daffodil Corridor near the staff room and its supply of tea and clean mugs. Instead, she found herself in Corridor Park. The Greek Chorus sat scowling at their needlework. Stella had seldom seen them look fiercer. Sally the Nodder held her little golden thread-snipping scissors before her face and snapped them open and shut upon the empty air.

The air was not all that was empty. For, next to Stella's seat under the skylight, Thelma's chair stood unoccupied.

A care worker might have taken Thelma to the washroom. Or … Stella tried to imagine where else Thelma might have gone. She could not. Thelma was limited in her movements, for nothing would stop her taking every opportunity to rest her hip and get well before anybody noticed the problem.

"Where is Thelma?" Stella asked.

"That young fellow took her off," Iolanthe said. "Thelma didn't want to."

"Want to what?"

"Go in the wheelchair he brought."

"That Riley *helped* her in," Lucille said. "Some help. Bumped her knee."

Stella steadied herself against her chair. "Where did Riley take Thelma?"

"Nowhere. Doctor Terry took her."

Iolanthe added, "He rolled her away, and she waved goodbye. That was not very much like our Thelma, was it?"

Stella swallowed. "How long ago?"

Iolanthe murmured, "It's hard to say, isn't it?"

Lucille nodded. "One minute is exactly like another."

"First, Dr Terry made a phone call, didn't he?"

"Oh, yes. For the ambulance."

Stella wanted to sit down in her chair so badly that her knees were doing it for her, but she straightened up. "Why didn't I see them in the corridor?"

"Oh, Stella, never knowing which way is up," Iolanthe sighed. "I suppose we all have to admit that it's about time Thelma had that hip of hers looked at, isn't it? But I did hate to see her go."

"If you don't want to be next off to hospital, Stella, take a load off your heart and give your rear to your chair," Lucille advised her. "Otherwise it could be you in the ambulance."

"True, true," Iolanthe hooted softly.

"Which way did Dr Terry take her?"

Lucille and Iolanthe glanced at one another. Before they could make a further reference to her poor directional instincts, Sally turned her gold scissors so that their sharp little points indicated her left and Stella's right. Stella set her sails, turned right, and hurried off along the corridor. Left, and then right. At this junction she ran straight into Reliza, who was travelling at a fast clip herself. Stella caught hold of Reliza's arms and steadied them both.

"I'm looking for Dr Terry," Stella said, thankful to have run into the one person in Fairmount who was in love with the doctor, for no matter how rocky the road of love might become, the young care worker was certain to know where in the building the doctor was. "I'm looking for him and for Thelma."

"You two are such friends." Sympathy shone from Reliza's bright eyes. "Did you not say goodbye?"

You mean au revoir, until we meet again. But this was no time for semantics. "No. Where can I find her? Where's the ambulance picking her up?"

"At the front door. I've just come from there. But I think …"

Stella didn't wait to see what Reliza thought. She headed at full speed in the direction from which Reliza had come. Straight on and then where? Some emergency-inspired sense of direction must have descended upon her like a gift from Olympus, for she turned right and found herself in the foyer, where she had recently stood among the women of Rose Corridor to watch Vaughn's big car pull away. Now Dr Terry stood alone with hands on hips at the foyer door, handsome and dog-tired as always. On the other side of the glass, at the end of Fairmount's laurel-edged walkway, an ambulance idled with open rear doors. An emergency worker in a white shirt with red piping on his collar slammed the doors shut and then peered inside the back windows.

The ambulance was too far away and at too narrow an angle for Stella to see what the emergency worker was looking at. But she knew: Thelma. Stella's great friend would be lying on the ambulance cot, strapped in for safety, small and silent as a fallen bird in her fleece suit and red silk slippers. She would be staring back at the emergency worker with her wise brown eyes. She would be terrified, but she would not show it.

The emergency worker secured the back lock of the double doors that shut Thelma inside. He tested the doors with a tug and disappeared around the far side of the vehicle. Stella knew that she had only seconds before he did what he was paid to do, *viz.* drive away with Thelma, likely never to return.

If only Stella could go too. But she knew it was useless to ask. Even Dr Terry, sweet as he could be when not too exhausted or lovelorn for good manners, wouldn't allow it. There were odd and sometimes mortal illnesses that elderly people caught in hospital, she knew, and there would be no place there for her to rest, sleep, or even sit and wait without a care worker. And anyway, nobody ever seemed to say *yes* at Fairmount.

Certainly, there was no time to argue.

If only she could have a stroke, she thought. They could bundle her in with Thelma in the back of the ambulance. Two birds, one bigger, one smaller, to be managed with one stone, if only she would fall senseless right this moment to the floor.

All this passed through Stella's mind in the second before she turned to Dr Terry.

He touched her shoulder. "Are you feeling well, Mrs Ryman?"

Unfortunately, yes.

But how was he to know? She drew down one side of her mouth and waved her right arm. She let her left arm dangle, the way they showed you in stroke awareness commercials on TV.

She fell to the floor, and heard her own fall rather than felt it. She lay on the gritty foyer tiles, the noise of Thelma's idling ambulance large in her head. She couldn't see the doctor or the ceiling above her. The little room turned grey and then black. Stella remembered with odd, swift logic, her wedding day so long ago. And she remembered her mother, Tanis Marie Seton, saying, *Be careful what you wish for, Stella, because there's always a catch.*

At the sound of the heavy click of a car door, Stella felt it was safe to open her eyes. She was lying along the back seat of a car, awkwardly strapped in place with a seat belt, her feet on the floor. She made out the top of the driver's curly head in the front seat.

She asked, "Where's Thelma?"

The driver didn't answer. Perhaps she hadn't asked the question out loud. She heard music, and understood that he was humming with the radio as he drove.

She twisted and pulled against her seat belt until she was able to sit up and see out the back window. The car was just pulling away from Fairmount's driveway and driving south. Thelma's ambulance was travelling north, heading downhill towards the first turning. It displayed its turning lights and disappeared around a corner.

"Follow that ambulance," Stella urged the driver. "Don't let it get away."

Riley spoke cheerfully from his spot at the wheel. "Don't you worry yourself, Mrs Ryman. I'll get you to hospital emergency in two shakes. The doctor phoned ahead for you, and he's sending you to the hospital a ways south of here, with the shortest waiting time for emergency."

Riley, too, put on his blinker. Stella closed her eyes and felt the turn take them farther from Thelma in her ambulance.

"Where are they taking Thelma? Why didn't they put me in her ambulance instead of you driving me?"

"She's going somewhere that does hips and legs, I guess," Riley said. "You're a different kettle of fish, medically speaking. But don't worry yourself, Mrs Ryman. It's my bet that a few days with the expert medicos will sort you out nicely."

Stella said hurriedly, "I feel better." But she did not feel better. She felt worse. Her heart pounded, and dizziness knocked her against the passenger door. She pulled herself up and tugged at her seat belt. "I feel a hundred percent better."

Riley didn't appear to have heard her. His indicator clicked again, and she leaned against the door as he took the next turn. She felt cold, despite the warm May noontide.

Outside the car windows, mansion gates flashed by, and a small beater of a car that must have belonged to a maid or caretaker pulled out in front of them. Riley merged into a long line of cars moving steadily away from Fairmount. *Be careful what you wish for, indeed.* Stella was outside now, wasn't she? She had tricked the doctor and escaped Fairmount. But here in Riley's power, she was less free than she had been before she pulled the stunt meant to reunite her with Thelma.

Those who leave Fairmount seldom return.

A green light ahead, at a busy crossing that Stella had never thought to see again, turned red. Riley swore and thumped on the brake. The light turned green again, and now Stella saw bridge rails flicker outside the car window.

She deduced that Riley was driving them south across the river. *What river?* Stella, attempting to recall the city's geography, thought of the River Styx. Riley was too handsome and feckless to make a good Charon. But then again, what did anybody know about the appearance or personal habits of the boatman of the River Styx? Only that one must pay to cross into the tunnels of the dead. One also recalled that, with few exceptions, no systems were set in place for a return journey from Hades.

She tucked her cold hands into her trouser pockets. There she found the lumped-up twenty- and hundred-dollar bills Vaughn had given her. *Charon's price, and more.* Outside, the river flashed sunlight, and she saw crows darting across a cloudless sky as the car sped southwards.

§

Will Stella convince her ferryman to turn around and follow Thelma Hu? Follow Stella's odyssey in Pulp Literature *Issue 39, Summer 2023.*

THE LABOURS OF MRS STELLA RYMAN
FURTHER FAIRMOUNT MANOR MYSTERIES

When the machineries of institution fail to protect Fairmount Manor, octogenarian amateur sleuth Mrs Stella Ryman rolls up her fleece jacket sleeves to ferret out a thief, investigate a gun-toting resident, set right a mishandled investigation of a man's death, pursue spectres and footpads walking at midnight, and discover Thelma Hu's long-lost fortune.

BOOK II OF THE FAIRMOUNT MANOR MYSTERIES BY MEL ANASTASIOU, AVAILABLE NOW FROM PULP LITERATURE PRESS

PULPLITERATURE.COM/STELLA-RYMAN
ISBN (PRINT): 978-1-988865-11-9
ISBN (EBOOK): 978-1-988865-12-6

ALL OUR SWAINS COMMEND HER

Mitchell Toews

Mitchell Toews lives and writes lakeside in the Manitoba boreal forest. His short fiction and creative nonfiction appear in print and online, in places near and far. A collection of short stories, Pinching Zwieback: Made-up Stories from the Darp (At Bay Press) is set for an autumn 2023 launch. His story 'Away Game' appeared in Issue 20, Autumn 2018. 'All Our Swains Commend Her' won second runner-up in our 2022 Raven contest. You may follow Mitch on the trails or out on the water or the ice, or more conveniently at Mitchellaneous.com, @mitchell_toews, bit.ly/MitchMastodon, and facebook.com/mitch.toews.

© 2023, Mitchell Toews

$\mathscr{A}$LL OUR SWAINS COMMEND HER

Nestor and I called her Ginger. She was the kind that tingles and burns. She'd been cadging coins down by the Country Kitchen every morning since this time last year. Loud and theatrical, Ginger was bigger than life. With a tin can for collecting money and a neatly lettered sign asking for donations, she'd escort slow-moving people on the crosswalk and always had a candy for little kids. It was Ginger's spot. Live street theatre in a raggedy Winnipeg Jets jacket.

We saw her every weekday on our commute. She was a fixture, standing at the intersection, skinny as a light pole. Orange eyebrows crept out from under her toque, matching the long locks that escaped her cap to lie in curls on her shoulders. Hair that was red once but was now the colour of her much-faded Nike Air Jordans.

Nestor asked her one time, "What's your background?" Her eyes locked on his, then mine.

"'Bout like you, I'd guess. Heinz 57, Manitoba style, as if I care, and you shouldn't neither. Don't you know? Multiculturalism is vested."

Comments like these made me think maybe her past was one of those that had a few zigs in it. Unlike mine, which had been straight-pipe middle class for generations. Nestor's was a little bumpier—his beginnings were the proverbial "humble." He had risen above his station, as he liked to say with a sardonic twist of the lip: he was loaded.

Ginger knew what we called her and seemed fine with it. Indifferent, anyway. I think she knew she was our pet conversation piece, something Nes and I shared and could talk about that wasn't sports or politics. She knew our names, and we had an easygoing street-corner relationship. Her finger would scold, tapping her wrist if we were late for our 7:40 pass-by each workday. We were like the hands on a clock for her, telling her where she was on her three-hour morning shift.

As we approached her corner, I toggled the control, sliding my window down a couple of inches. The air was filled with the nasty burnt smell internal combustion engines produce in the cold. Focusing on the road ahead, I could make Ginger out in the exhaust fog. She stood out like a six-foot channel marker at the confluence of the crowded intersection. Like most mornings, she was there at her post, come storm or siege. I admired her for this gutsy way of living through a Winnipeg winter. Pretty sure I could not pull it off. My white-collar job was tedious and I had to suffer idiots in silence, but it was indoors, safe, and it paid reasonably well.

Nestor's minty, sapphire-blue BMW was his baby. A rust-free '91 four-door, imported from Phoenix at significant expense. This car, in Nestor's complicated view, went a step beyond showing off. He considered himself "generally immune to hubris" because of his hardscrabble early days. "Anything I have now, I earned." A new Beamer would have been ostentatious and bougie, but this scrupulously maintained, vintage beauty sidestepped all that ignominy. Or so he claimed.

"A properly maintained luxury car will run forever, so it's better economically and environmentally," Nestor preached at me every other Friday as we sat in the car wash queue after work. "But rust eats it. It's the salt on our winter roads. No salt on Arizona highways … not a lick."

He was right of course, but I knew the speech by heart, like the Lord's Prayer: *"Thou shalt select the deluxe undercarriage wash cycle …"*

I had my own dubious transportation perspective. I drove guilt-free in my old car, although I did not ride the bus, as Nestor was quick to point out. I saw myself as a Bolshevik plebe in my unassuming commuter car. It was a "real beater," as my dad would have called it, and he would have avoided being seen in it. Times change. I believed the two contrasting cars—mine and Nestor's—were representative of the differences in our present-day characters. Kind of a flip-flop from when we were growing up and I was middle-class while Nestor was … not.

Besides letting me feel like I wasn't all that privileged, my humble worker's wheels left me unafraid of the punishing Manitoba winter. Dented and trimmed with lacy rust, my ride was made of Windsor—not Bavarian—sheet metal. My pride was in practicality. My winter wagon ran smooth as cat shit and started in any weather, but trendy it was not. Not even shabby chic.

Nestor and I had a system figured out: driver's car, driver's rules. Radio stations, temperature, intermittent wiper speed, even panhandlers. Nestor would dismiss certain street-corner windshield washers with a bark—"Hands off the car!"—and send them and their sloshing ice-cream pails of turd-brown water to scratch someone else's windows. But when we got to Ginger's corner, Nestor always insisted we each contribute a loonie. He kept his reasons to himself except for the occasional grunted observation that I "wouldn't miss it" or that it was a tenth of what I spent on take-out coffee every day. Driver makes the rules, so I didn't object. It seemed obvious to me that Nestor's thin beginnings — as a poor kid from the North End who made it into university on a full academic scholarship — were at the root of his patronage of Ginger.

On my days to drive, like today, when we arrived at Ginger's roost, I stared straight ahead while Nestor fidgeted in his pockets for coins. Finding none, he fingered my parking meter stash in the console. "I'll pay you back," he said with a glare, both of us knowing he wouldn't bother.

"She'll just spend it on dope …" I said, baiting him with redneck chapter-and-verse.

Nestor scoffed at me, his high and his mighty jostling for position. "Just give the money and don't worry about the results. Don't let society tut-tut in your head. The charity, Wallace, is in your intent. If it'll help your generosity, why don't you take a picture of Ginger, all hoary and whatnot, and put it up in your cubicle? Add a caption like, 'There but for the grace of God' or something like that."

Bite me, I thought, but kept my mouth shut. It wasn't that he was wrong, just that it was all a bit too performative for my liking. Too much a segue into his whole rags-to-riches brand, which was about ready for a reset in my view.

Outside on the median beside the car, Ginger lifted one cold foot, then the other, as if marching in time. Her exhale was an ivory plume, and thick frost ringed her mouth, like a seal breathing-hole in the ice.

"Her Nikes don't look too warm," Nestor said, holier than thou. A little pissy.

"I had a pair of shoes like that in high school," I said, trying for a new topic. "Best runners ever. Wore them in the provincials. Remember?"

"Yep. I was jealous. No way I could afford a pair. How'd you manage, anyway?"

"Christmas."

Nes had been a smooth-stroking point guard, captain of our school team. Quiet and reedy—a natural shooter. Surprisingly tough, too, back then. No bullshit. I remember him protecting a rebound with elbows high, swinging them to make room. Then the guy guarding him was on the floor, bellowing through bloody fingers, "You broke my fuggin' nose!"

He was paunchy now. "I'm yoga fit. I don't give a shit about three-pointers anymore, Wallace," he always said. Laconic. Full of himself.

Ginger waved at Nestor as we pulled away. She only barely nodded at me—a little uncertain of how the parts fit together between me and Nes. Lately, that made two of us.

Next day was warmer, and the sand trucks had been out—less slipping and sliding—but the radio warned of heavy traffic. It had been a long winter with more to come, and I felt a little sorry for myself as I scraped the windshield.

Nestor and I drove without much conversation. He busied himself with some spreadsheets. At Ginger's corner, we sat several cars back of the light. She was chewing on an enormous chocolate bar someone had given her. As we approached, crawling along, she finished eating and tossed the wrapper into the road.

"Smooth move, Ginger. For shit's sakes . . ." I muttered.

She must have read my lips. With a sneer, she looked at me through the windshield, mouthed back, "For shit's sakes," pouted, then flashed a chocolate-toothed grin and waved to Nestor.

"Morning, Nestor!" we heard her holler.

"Poverty is the greatest polluter," Nestor proclaimed from the passenger seat. He had a point there, and he should know. He's the same guy who used to stick flyers under windshield wipers for lunch money, dumping most of them into the Red River down at the tail end of Pritchard Avenue.

"Oh, great," I said as the light changed and my daydream ended. I was caught with my northbound front end in the eastbound lane. Oncoming cars honked. The ultimate commuter's badge of shame—I was blocking traffic. To my rescue, Ginger jumped behind our car and waved her thin arms.

"Back up, youse guys! Give him some *room*, eh?" she shouted, her voice impossibly high. Then she pivoted on a Nike sole, crouched, and rolled her hand at me like she was winding a fishing reel, staring intently at my beat-up bumper as I crept back. She yelled, "Ho!" and gave me an 'okay' signal in the mirror when I was snuggled up to the car behind us.

I cracked my window and slid a loonie into Ginger's waiting mitt. She snickered, tossed the coin in the air, and caught it in the wool basket of her two hands. "Pleasure doin' business witcha, Wally . . ." she said with a dimpled grin and a wink. "Nice to see you got religion!"

Nestor snorted, not looking up from his work.

"Not religion—capitalism," I replied to Ginger through the slit of open window, ignoring Nestor. "Money paid for service rendered."

"Well, for once we agree, hombre. Good to see you're catching on to how life works out here in the frost zone."

The cross-traffic ahead of us began to move again, but then their light changed to red. A delivery van got trapped in the same way I just had. Horns blared. We were woven together, cars pointing in all directions, tailpipes spewing thin white columns up through the windless air like campfire smoke.

"Here we go. Gridlock." Nestor set aside his spreadsheet.

We watched as Ginger ran out into the snarled intersection in front of us and took control. She was a Disney animatronic traffic cop, arms churning. Pedestrians cheered, and her cash can tinkled more than a few times.

The traffic flowed and Ginger, triumphant and filled with the spirit of the moment, took off her Jets jacket to let the last car through, matador style. She yelled, "Ha! Toro!"

As the car went by, the passenger leaned out of his window and snatched her jacket.

"Get a job, loser!" the driver yelled, and floored it, laughing, spraying Ginger with a mixture of salt, gravel, and slush. As the car drove onto the bridge, Ginger watched until it topped the hump at the centre and disappeared into the whiteness beyond. Walking slowly, she returned to the median.

The traffic signal changed and the vehicle behind me honked, but before I could get going Nestor yelled, "Hold it!" and jumped out of the car. His upraised arm stopped traffic and brought on a brassy medley—steady oboes and B-flat Toyotas. He jogged over to her and I opened my window to listen.

"Here, Ginger. Please," he said, sliding his car coat off. "Take this." The cacophony ceased. *Showboat*, I thought.

Ginger gave Nestor a baleful, three-beat stare. With a sniff, she shifted her gaze up the road to where her jacket had disappeared. Bending slowly, she picked up her money can with one crooked finger and walked, like the Queen at her coronation, across the street. Coming to a ceremonious halt in the middle of the road in the snow-muffled silence, she filled her lungs and bawled, in an oddly melodious and musical soprano,

> *"I'm burly and brawny,*
> *My hair's rather tawny,*
> *and if you don't like me*
> *that's tough.*
>
> *I shit thunder and lightning,*
> *and everything frightening,*
> *and where I come from*
> *that's enough."*

Bleating horns sounded at a distance, but close by, all was still except for some mittened applause from waiting pedestrians. Ginger acknowledged her audience with a flourishing bow and continued, facing Nestor, who stood now on the median, coat over his arm.

"Fella, my name is Sylvia Roundtree, not Ginger — which, by the by, is a name I can't friggin' *stand*. And, also, I earned this money." She jingled the can convincingly — it was heavy with loonies and toonies. "I provide a valuable service at this corner. I will buy myself a jacket with this here money. Thanks for the offer, but you should give your stinkin' coat to someone who don't have a job and who needs the charity. That ain't me. And remember this, Nestor: 'one may smile, and smile, and be a villain.'"

With that, Sylvia flipped him a big-knuckled middle finger, delivered underhand like a scoop lay-up on a breakaway. I was about to let loose with a victorious, "Yes!" but then I saw Nestor's face as he turned slowly, slipping the rejected coat back on. He looked like he had caught himself breaking a promise he had made once and since forgotten. I set aside my pettiness and wondered about the things Nestor and I had chosen to find important that winter. She gave us her back and ambled across the street, detouring to accept a bright-blue fiver from a waiting taxi driver. With a step up on the far curb, she disappeared forever into the surge of cars and people and the rising white exhaust haze.

OLYMPIAN

FJ Bergmann

FJ Bergmann is the poetry editor of Mobius: The Journal of Social Change (mobiusmagazine.com) and freelances as a copy editor and book designer. She lives in Wisconsin and fantasizes about tragedies on or near exoplanets. She is a Writers of the Future winner. Her work has appeared in Abyss & Apex, Analog, Asimov's SF, and elsewhere in the alphabet. While lacking academic literary qualifications, she is kind to those so encumbered. She used to work with horses. She thinks imagination can compensate for anything. This is her fourth appearance in Pulp Literature, and you can find her previous stories, 'Opening Doors', 'For Your Convenience', and 'Yellow Paint', in issues 6, 16, and 24 respectively.

© 2023, FJ Bergmann

Olympian

Festivities were in full swing. An orchestra of timpani, syrinxes, harps, and kitharas blared from a corner of the temple, echoing among the fluted pillars, while hooves and sandals clattered on the marble floor, mingling with uplifted voices and the thudding of bare feet and paws. In the centre of the naos, a fountain gushed dark wine. It was Dionysus's birthday, and he had chosen to manifest as a baby: an infernal nuisance of a chubby infant, sitting in the fountain (without a diaper), swilling wine, and grabbing at every exposed breast he saw, no matter how virginal. His entourage of fauns and maenads swirled about the fountain, dancing frenetically, grinning, grinding their hips against each other, and occasionally plunging their faces into the fountain to rise back up with dripping, purple-stained lips.

I stood in the shadows of the adyton under the towering statue of Nemesis, resting a hind leg and fanning myself with my wings as I watched the celebrants stumble into each other. The day had been a scorcher, and no breeze had yet brought respite, though the Winds had been invited and offerings made to them. A centaur tried to trot through a puddle of wine on the floor, and his hindquarters slid out from under him as he brayed in dismay. Horses are more split-brained than humans — and that fellow was quite split-brained, even for a part-horse.

I am *all* horse, of course. Jealous folk cast aspersions on me by claiming I must be part bird (usually vulture or chicken), but my wings are a purely divine attribute that I owe to my father, Poseidon. What I owe to my mother, Medusa, I could not say; she died as I was being born, and whatever she contributed to my person is not visible.

I no longer have a rider nor owe allegiance to any human or being save the immortal gods — some of them, anyway. Bellerophon eventually overfaced me, as so many riders do, by setting me at Olympus. And I reacted appropriately, as so many horses do. He fell a long way.

I could speak of pride and hubris, but I have learned to attach little importance to adages and proverbs. In the end, all are piled for burning. It is difficult to stay sane when the gods constantly demand labours and we are given no rest before being sent out again on a task at their divine whims. And even the gods go mad at times, as Dionysus has shown us often before.

The sun was going down; the temple pillars gradually darkened from silver to gold to bronze as night fell and starved them of light. Though still unmoving, the air was beginning to cool. One of the most drunken dancing women, spinning dizzily, staggered within range of Dionysus, and he took her by the arm and held her against him while his followers chanted encouragement. In the course of the evening he had changed from an infant to a rather handsome youth, if you like that sort of thing. Humans imbibe wine for many reasons, some for debauchery, some out of desperation. She struggled to escape his grasp as he thrust his loins against her, giggling. His entourage began to whoop in unison.

Doing something willingly is one thing; having it done to one is another matter. I began to walk toward them, my wings continuing to slowly open and close.

Still gripping her arm, he pulled up her robe (he himself wore nothing but wine stains) and backed her against the fountain's lip. I curled my neck between them and nudged him rather abruptly.

"Whaddaya think yer doin', horse?" He turned on me, and the god-light in his eyes began to redden with rage.

"Ever done it flying?" I said. I gave a neighing horse-laugh and nudged him again. "Bet that would be something to boast about to Zeus, hey?"

For a moment I thought he would smite me, but slowly the red light died, and he grinned. "Good one, Pegasus!" He turned back to the woman. "Get up there!" he said to her—maenad, nymph, whoever she was—and threw her up onto my back, scrambling up after her.

We rose into the night sky, and my strong wingbeats took us out over the sea. I was pleased to note that she had a death grip on my mane. A touch of acrophobia can do wonders with regard to sobering up. As Dionysus took hold of her robe again, I twitched my rump ever so slightly ... *He* was still very drunk indeed.

The fall wouldn't kill him (another divine attribute), and with any luck, he wouldn't remember what had happened when he woke the following day.

"Where to?" I asked my remaining rider.

WAFFLES AND STRAWBERRIES

Susan Alexander

Susan Alexander *is the author of two collections of poems,* Nothing You Can Carry *and* The Dance Floor Tilts, *both with Thistledown Press. Her work has won multiple awards, most recently Vancouver's City Poems Contest in June 2022. Her poems appear in anthologies and literary magazines in Canada, the UK, and the US and have ridden the bus as part of Poetry in Transit. She lives on Nexwlélexm/Bowen Island, BC, on the traditional and unceded territory of the Squamish people.*

© 2023, Susan Alexander

Waffles and Strawberries

When he gives me the news, I'm slicing
strawberries for waffles because lately
he seems far away and even though
he'd never ask, I know what he loves.
I'm thinking of my Norwegian grandmother
who had ten to feed, my mum with seven
and there would've been more if she hadn't
persuaded the surgeon to tie her tubes
when he removed half her ulcered stomach —
at least that's how I heard the story.

> The old recipe pasted inside
> a makeshift cookbook, its spine broken,
> loose sheets gathered by a rubber band.

When he gives me the news, I've already
whisked the egg whites, folded their peaks
into batter and ladled it over the checkers.
His bone marrow hatching something
called blasts which explains why

he's so tired. We've stopped reaching
for each other. He says it feels like
a performance I demand, but it isn't
that way at all, just how I blush when
he touches me with those powerful hands.

    O the strenuous wait! That infinite delay!
    The sudden gold I love to break into
    perfect hearts, sweetness filling each hollow.

No more cast iron on the stovetop
like Grammy who served hers
with whipped cream and preserves,
though with Mum it was simpler,
butter and so-called syrup —
boiled sugar water, flavoured
with Mapleine. A distant beep.
I smell the hot bake. I offer him
waffles with everything,

    butter and real maple syrup,
    heavy cream and strawberries,
    because that's the way they taste best.

It's winter now so even though
every trucked-in berry promises sweet
under ruby skin, each slice
pales to white.

PSYCHOPOMPS ARE US

Melanie Marttila

Always looking up, eyes on the skies, head in the clouds, #actuallyautistic author **Melanie Marttila** *writes poetry and speculative tales of hope in the face of adversity. She lives and writes in Sudbury, Ontario, in the house where three generations of her family have lived, on the street that bears her surname, with her spouse and their dog, Torvi.*

© 2023, Melanie Marttila

$\mathcal{P}$SYCHOPOMPS ARE US

The attendants lower you into the Kerning[1] Couch. You are rigid and wild-eyed, but they don't bother to reassure you. There will be muscle relaxants and twilight sedatives administered in another moment.

A cap with sensors is snugged into place over your shaved head to monitor your beautiful, special brain, without which you could not do this work. Nasal prongs follow, and more sticky pads and clips to monitor heartbeat, pulse, oxygen, and temperature. The Psychopomp Corps[2] obsess over the physical wellbeing of their operatives.[3]

You're holding up well, keeping that chin stiff, but your eyes give you away: too much white showing, pupils reduced to dots. Your arms remain relaxed when the attendants insert the

[1] The Necropolis thinks they're being clever by naming the space between life and death after the space between printed characters.

[2] I've never understood why they don't add an *e* to the end of *Corps*.

[3] Your mental health? That's what the counsellors are for. Later. When you've returned.

intravenous, and the first drips have no noticeable effect. But then your eyelids flutter and your tension falls away. You fall away. It won't be long now.

Your astral form consolidates in the bedroom of Kristina Blonski, who died in her sleep from a brain aneurysm.[4]

You orient, focusing on the cheap floral comforter and matching curtains, the refinished highboy, vanity, and chest — old but not antique — and the still body in the bed.

Kristina's spirit sweeps up behind you. "Who the hell are you, and what are you doing in my room?"

You quell a start, swallow a gasp. Those responses belong to your body. You struggle to leave it and its reactions in the living world and rotate to face your assigned spirit. "Kristina Blonski?"

"Answer my question." She leans down, in your face almost literally.

You tingle where spirit touches astral body. "I'm your guide to the afterlife."

"Not going." Kristina punches you, and you shudder as her fist passes through your head with the sensation of lightning.

You straighten, unable to hide your disappointment that your astral form is limited to the dimensions of your real body, which you think of as short and fat and inadequate.[5] You run through the scripts you were taught, pick one that should work. "Your family is waiting for you. George is waiting."

It's not exactly a lie. They could be there.[6]

---

[4] I'll leave it to you to determine whether it was peaceful or not.

[5] It is none of those things, I assure you.

[6] None of us still living knows for sure what lies beyond the veil.

Kristina rolls her eyes. "Why did you have to send such a newbie?" she asks the ceiling before focusing her attention on you. "I don't know what dry facts you have on me, but you're missing some important information."[7]

There are contingencies for feisty or reluctant spirits. Get her to talk about herself. "Why don't you fill me in, then, Kristina?"

"Oho!" she crows. "Now you want me to do your job for you?"

You pull your stomach in, away from the warning tingle of Kristina's spirit, stand your ground, and look up at her. "My job is to see you to the afterlife."

"Whatever helps you sleep." Kristina sweeps back to her bedside again, back to her still-cooling corpse. "My family thinks I'm aberrant. My marriage wasn't a love match."

"Death has a habit of changing perspective, though. You might be surprised."

"What if I don't care to be surprised?"

You can't force a spirit to cross over. They have to go willingly. Kristina has a reason to stick around. "What, or should I say who, do you care for, then?"

You're not supposed to deviate from the script. Admittedly, it's difficult to play the grimmest of grim reapers when you look like someone who dispenses hugs to everyone they meet, but you should at least try. You don't have time to mess around.[8]

---

[7] To their credit, Records handles the lives of every person who's ever lived since our earliest hominid ancestors. Dry facts are probably all they have time for these days.

[8] Psychopomps have until the next dawn to see their appointed spirits into the afterlife. Because Kristina died at three in the morning, you have less time than most.

Kristina lifts her chin and looks down her nose at you. "Gerry," she says, like you should know who that is.

"And where is Gerry?"

There's victory in Kristina's smile. "Follow me."

You move through walls, the electrical wiring pulling both spirit and astral bodies this way and that. Uncomfortable is a mild term for it. You're still in the same building, just three rooms over, when Kristina slows to hover over a shrivelled figure in a wheelchair.

Gut twisting, you decide to take note of the name and address of this nursing home when you have a chance. There's work to be done in the living world. After you see Kristina to the other side.

"Gerry," she says, her voice the loving caress she's no longer capable of.

You crouch to get a good look at the person in the chair, and the scent of waste hits your nose like a fist. You run your insubstantial hands over Gerry's body, notice other signs of neglect, and finally plunge your hands into her. You wince at the violation, but it's the only way, in astral form, you can learn anything about a living person.[9] You withdraw.

Gerry is short for Geraldine.

"What do you propose to do?" you ask.

"I'm staying with Gerry until she can come with me."

It's true that poor Gerry isn't long for this world, but she has enough life left in her to last a few more days. Will Kristina believe you if you tell her what will happen if she doesn't willingly pass into the afterlife before the sun rises? She'll probably think you're trying to scare her into compliance. If only that would work. "And what will you do while you're waiting?"

---

[9] It's a variety of psychometry.

"She'll know I'm here."

"Will she, though?" Being soul mates in life doesn't necessarily mean a bond beyond death. You want Kristina to try, though, to see the futility of lingering. You tap your insubstantial lips with an equally insubstantial finger.

"Like you know anything, newbie." Kristina reaches for Gerry's shoulders, but stops, frowning, when her hands pass through her lover's body. She retreats and tries again, grimacing, like will alone can restore her ability to make contact.

You know enough to be patient. For a little longer.

Kristina fails to touch Gerry three more times. Then she speaks, softly at first, eventually shouting. Gerry doesn't move. The only sound she makes is a shuddering huffle on the exhale, her slack lips quivering on uneven breath.

"What have you done to me?" Kristina wails. She charges you but passes bodily through.

The numbing buzz of an electrical shock leaves you stunned. You rally, turn to face Kristina. "You're a spirit, not a ghost, and even if you were a ghost, it's not like it is in the stories. You don't just step out of your body and have a whole new set of skills. You have to learn them. It takes time and a lot of it."

"How do I become a ghost?" she demands.

"You're well on your way. Keep up with the stubborn until the sun rises, and you'll become a ghost. You'll feel it happen. I've been told it's like a second death, though you'll be the first spirit whose transition I witness. You won't be able to pass into the afterlife then, even if you want to. Even if Gerry does when she dies in a few days, you won't be able to follow her. You'll be stuck here, and you'll have all the time in the world to learn how to be a first-class ghost."

"Liar!"

You fist your hands on your hips and strike a pose with as much attitude as your astral form can project.

Kristina fumes, frowns, pouts, dithers in three different directions, and finally stares down at you again. "I'll tell Gerry to stay with me."

You shake your head. "I'm sorry if I wasn't clear. Spirits and ghosts are two different entities. I'm afraid Gerry's spirit won't understand your ghost any more than Gerry can understand your spirit now."

Kristina howls and attacks again.

You repress the urge to flinch this time, letting Kristina do her worst.[10]

You move back — in the guise of dodging. One step, two, through the first wall, and onward. Or backward. Kristina's spirit is so focused on trying to beat you down that she doesn't even notice.

Until you're corpse-side.

"Bitch." Though the epithet seems to be directed at you, Kristina's gaze is fused to the body on the bed.

"You have a choice," you say. "Cross over by sunrise and have the chance to greet Gerry when she does the same in a few days — or stay here, become a ghost, and never be able to touch or speak to her again."

You walk to the window and, though you think it looks ridiculous, stick your head through the curtains. "Sun's almost up." You feel the sands in Kristina's hourglass running out and think of how you'll teach the psychopomp curriculum

---

[10] Aside from the stunning side effects, she can't permanently damage your astral body.

differently, how you might find the time to incorporate a few cogent details in Records, or how you'll probably have to go back to school in the living world. Maybe palliative care? Grief counselling? Mortician? You can't remember if you had the grades to support the medical school necessary to become a coroner. None of it feels as right to you as being a psychopomp, though.

And then Kristina's face pokes through the curtains beside you. Her sigh rises from the depths of her spirit. "All right, then. Let's go."

You step back and so does she. You don't know how to do this part. No one ever showed you how.[11] You're in a deer-in-the-headlights panic.

"Well?"

Kristina's question shakes you into action. What have you got to lose? You touch Kristina, focus on the zing of electricity. The afterlife calls to all the dead, even if they ignore it. Even if they don't want to go. You breathe, sink into Kristina's spirit, find that place that is not a place where the yearning resides. Finally, you feel a pull. A push. A direction and destination. "Follow me."

You don't go anywhere, but the room grows hazy. Kristina becomes a ball of light. Then, the world around you is gone and everything fades into blinding white.

"Krissy!" It's a woman's voice.

"Ani Li?" Kristina's whisper is full of wonder. "I—"

And you're pulled violently back, out of the white, away from Kristina's corpse, and into your physical body.

"That was close, don't you think?"

---

[11] One of the limitations of Necropolis University. All theory, no practice.

You cut your eyes at the woman dressed in an examiner's violet robes.[12]

"Get on with the getting on next time."

You bite your tongue.[13]

"Anyway, congratulations are in order. You've passed your final practical exam."

The examiner leans down and tucks an amulet[14] into the folds of your blanket.

"Welcome to the Psychopomp Corpse."[15]

[12] You might be comforted to know what I'm wearing beneath the robes. Or not.

[13] Thanks for that. I might have been tempted to deduct marks for snark.

[14] You'll find out what it does when you put it on. I want to be there when you do.

[15] Did I say that?

THE LEAST OF MYSELF

Sylvia Leong

Sylvia Leong is an emerging writer, passionate environmentalist, and therapeutic personal trainer living in a shoebox in the sky in North Vancouver. When she's not hiking the rainforest, snapping photos, and searching for fairies, she's snuggled in bed with her laptop, revising her third novel or drafting her fourth. Sylvia's piece 'Ghost Story' appeared in Pulp Literature Issue 29. You can find her at slleong.com.

© 2023, Sylvia Leong

$\mathscr{T}$HE LEAST OF MYSELF

The cracks between the cobblestones chewed the heels of my gold-coloured stilettos. I lifted to the balls of my feet, wincing at the stabbing pain, and walked through the ornate gates into a dim courtyard strung with fairy lights. A crimson bulb illuminated the stone staircase up to the restaurant. The same restaurant we'd dined in earlier.

A black hump lay at the foot of the stairs. One step forward. A pile of something? One more step. No, a human. Another step. A woman.

A normal person would run to her. A good person would check her pulse. I stood still as a gravestone.

Just fifteen minutes ago, I'd navigated my way down that staircase in my six-inch heels, marvelling at the steepness, thighs straining like a tightrope walker, and gripping the wrought-iron railing as though my life depended on it. Signs posted at the top and the bottom read *Caution, Watch your Step, At Own Risk.*

There was no blood, at least none that I could see. The woman lay belly down, neck turned, head resting like she'd collapsed. One of her legs was straight and the other was bent, as though she were asleep on crisp sheets in a warm bed.

Maybe she was asleep. Just so, so tired.

That's ridiculous, said the little voice in the back of my head, the little voice that was the least of myself.

We were both blonde, her hair curly and coming loose from its pins. My hair was longer, thicker, straighter. My legs were sculpted from years of ballet. Was I prettier? Probably.

Just a step closer and I'd be able to see her face.

But I wouldn't just see *her* face. I would also see my mom's.

After my parents' airplane crashed into the Atlantic, I dreamt of the accident almost every night: sometimes as a movie reel in vignettes, other times more vivid than reality. Always, oxygen masks springing from the ceiling. A yellow plastic cup coming at my face. Flying purses and books, tumbling laptops and pillows. My mother's left hand—gold wedding band with a small diamond between tiny blue sapphires—grasping my father's hand, larger and darker. The armrest beneath vibrating violently. Knuckles turning white. Screaming. A sickening jolt. A wall of water with flames dancing along the edges. Black.

My parents were never found. But in my mind, I saw their mangled bodies everywhere: floating in the ocean, lying on the beach, reclining on chaises longues on an apartment balcony, stretching on the hardwood floor of the ballet studio. I knew none of it was real. But try telling that to my quickened pulse, my shallow breaths, my frozen limbs.

Gawd! **What was wrong with me?** I needed to help her. Or go get help.

My stomach clenched at the thought of touching her, of even going near her.

We were the same, the woman and I. Sugar babies luring in sugar daddies. She wore the costume. My dress was gold lamé, a Michael Kors. Hers was silver and slate. A Ferretti?

The silky fabric draped over the top of her thigh, high enough to expose her shapely legs, low enough to preserve her dignity. Straight men would see it as effortlessly sexy. To me it looked like she'd slyly rearranged it after her fall.

I could brush past to the stairs, careful not to touch her. I couldn't just stand here.

Hot guilt trickled down my spine. Would she join my parents, returning to flicker in my mind like a neon sign?

She'd already ruined what had been a magical night.

But it wasn't magical, said the least of myself.

My date had brought me here, gushing about the restaurant renovation, calling it modern and innovative. It occupied both floors of the historical building, and a blue-windowed skyscraper wrapped around it on two sides. Everything he needed was right here: the restaurant where everyone knew his name, his penthouse high above in the skyscraper, and his office on a lower floor. A shrunken world. A toddler confined to a playpen.

"The commute kills me," he'd joked. *Original.* But at least he'd made an attempt. Most corporate types got what they wanted without bothering with humour.

I had smiled, hiding my disdain, telling myself, *It's just as easy to marry a rich man as a poor one.* Didn't Marilyn Monroe say something like that? Or maybe it was *fall in love with*, not *marry.*

Silly woman. Love was a fool's myth. But marriage came with money.

He'd shown me his office, all walnut panelling and windows. With gentle intensity, he'd pushed me down on his charcoal-coloured desk, lifting one of my long legs over his shoulder, my other toe just reaching the floor, lace panties dangling from my ankle.

The streetlamp shone through the window, brightening his white shirt and white tie. A speck of burgundy lasagne sauce smudged the tip of his collar. Later, he'd be sorry about that. Or maybe he owned so many shirts he wouldn't care.

His suit was steel blue. Gorgeous, unusual, artful, making me think that maybe we had a chance. Belt undone, he fumbled with the button of his pants.

My hips lifted, aching, anticipating.

Instead, he moved back, brows furrowing, lowering my leg to the desk. "Not in my office. Not this time."

This time. This time. This time. Was there a possibility of commitment here?

"Upstairs will be more discreet," he said, clasping my hand and pulling me up.

Discreet? I deflated.

"I just need to wrap up one thing." He buttoned his pants and began to shuffle through the files on his desk.

"I'll run and use the bathroom back at the restaurant."

He laughed. "My penthouse comes fully equipped with a washroom."

But I wanted a moment apart from him. High-powered men love the thrill of the chase. I needed to pull back, regain my mystique, trigger his hunter's mentality. The greater his effort, the higher my value.

"I'll only be a second," I said, "while you do what you need to do."

Now, the savoury tang of tomato, beef, and cheese wafted down from the restaurant. A motorcycle roared past the courtyard, its loose cough fading into the distance.

She looked cold. Not that she'd ever have to worry about being cold again. Someone would come upon her long before the heat left her body.

I stepped back, a thousand hot needles again piercing my feet. Another step, and another, until my bare shoulder blades pressed against the rough coolness of the courtyard's brick wall, and I tucked into the shadows.

Why did *I* have to interrupt my night to deal with this? Later I might be sitting beneath harsh overhead lights, at a stainless steel table, in an air-conditioned room, rubbing the backs of my arms, defending myself—*I panicked, that's all.*

I could still duck out, walk away, forget her. *My penthouse comes fully equipped with a washroom.* His penthouse was probably like his office: shadowy, sleek, masculine . . . warm. He'd offer more wine.

Self-serving, said the least of myself.

I brushed my fingers down my throat. How long had I been standing here? What if he'd "wrapped up that one thing"? The courtyard was the only way in or out of the restaurant. He'd look for me here and find me. Find me doing nothing to help her.

What if she was taking her last breaths? A decent person would rush over. Call 911. That I could do.

My gold-sequined Alexander McQueen purse hung on its chain from my shoulder. An expensive gift from a former conquest. I turned the little gold skull clasp and pulled out my phone.

My hand trembled over the lit screen. My finger couldn't land on the numbers to unlock my phone.

Voices. Footsteps. Walking past the courtyard? Or coming through? My heart punched my ribs.

Five people crowded beneath the arched entranceway. A man turned and glanced over his shoulder. He looked straight into my face.

"I was just about to call 911," I said.

My phone went dark.

One of the women screamed a horror-movie scream, fake, like she wasn't sure about the appropriate response.

Two other women rushed over.

"She's still breathing," one shrilled.

"Don't move her," someone bellowed, "in case of a spinal injury."

I drooped as the yoke of responsibility seemed to fall from my shoulders.

The man looking at me said, "Are you calling 911, or what?"

My heart stuttered. "Uh …" I tilted my phone. "Battery just went dead."

In the dimness of the courtyard, his eyes were an indeterminable pale colour. But they hardened as surely as the line of his mouth. He knew I was lying, understood exactly what kind of person I was, saw through me to the least of myself.

Bile filled the back of my mouth. He hadn't exactly run to the fallen woman's side either, had he? No, he'd stood back, pinning me with his stare, while his friends, noble and humane, took action. I lifted my chin. Who was *he* to make judgments about *me*?

I flicked my hair over my shoulder and whirled towards the archway. Avoiding the cracks between the cobblestones, I ignored the electric pain in my feet and walked out of the courtyard.

My date was waiting.

THE JACK WHYTE STORYTELLER AWARD

Mike Carson

Mike Carson is living proof of Douglas Adams's aphorism, "It takes an awful lot of time to not write a book." In his years of literary procrastination and steady weight gain, however, Mike has managed to publish several short stories and essays, win a few writing awards, and survive 33 years as a high school teacher. He lives in Kamloops with his wife and family, and is still teaching and working away at not writing a book. 'Andouille' was chosen by judge Diana Gabaldon as the second runner-up of the Surrey International Writers' Conference 2022 Jack Whyte Storyteller Award, and Mike is honoured to have another of his winning entries published in Pulp Literature. His story 'Deep Water', also a Storyteller Award runner-up, appeared in Issue 26, Spring 2020.

© 2023, Mike Carson

$\mathcal{A}$NDOUILLE

Perhaps it was a stirring of heartfelt compassion for the far-off country of his birth that compelled Monsieur Boucher, in the fall of 1915, to offer up his only son to the Great War. A more plausible motive for his decision, however — and the prevalent theory held by those few who had sounded the shallow depths of the man's heart — was M. Boucher's recent remarriage. Having divested himself of the former Madame Boucher (God rest her soul) who succumbed to a fever contracted, or so M. Boucher attested, due to her inability to keep her mouth shut even when surrounded by contagion, Monsieur Boucher had apparently been inspired to make a clean sweep of the rest of his family. M. Boucher no doubt felt he would have better luck producing a son of work ethic and intelligence with Judit, the new, younger, and far less loquacious Madame Boucher.

Indeed, any residents of the remote community of Norway House who concerned themselves with the domestic affairs of their neighbours — which is to say the majority of them — conceded that producing even one heir with M. Boucher could only have been achieved under a shroud of darkness or a fume of whiskey. Still, there was no shortage of either during the long

Manitoba winters. Norway House was a cold place — anyone would tell you that — and hard on those whose dreams exceeded the reach of a saw blade or fishing line.

Albert — the aforementioned 'rest' of M. Boucher's family — was sitting in the woodshed, sketching in a tattered notebook, when his father arrived to inform him of the good news that he was to be afforded the honour of dying — perhaps even gloriously — for *la belle France*. Perched above them, Andouille the pigeon (Albert's intellectual equal, according to M. Boucher), flapped an unheeded warning.

The former Madame Boucher had found the young pigeon and given it to Albert to raise. Even if any of the family had been more ornithologically minded, no one could have blamed them for failing to recognize that Andouille was a passenger pigeon, whose existence in the wilds of Manitoba — or anywhere, for that matter — was nothing short of miraculous: the birds, whose multitudinous flocks once darkened the skies, had been hunted to extinction. In 1914, in fact, it was widely reported that the last passenger pigeon in North America, a bedraggled old bird called Martha, spared from birdshot and stew pot by protective incarceration at the Cincinnati Zoo, had at last moulted up her ghost.

What divine winds blew Andouille to Norway House and into the keeping of one lonely boy, only the winds themselves can say. Still, somehow a nesting pair had reached this lead-free haven in defiance of the instinct that had drawn untold millions of their kind back to the banks of Mimico Creek each year and into the gun sights of Toronto's upper classes.

It was M. Boucher who suggested the name Andouille, although he failed to provide its meaning for his wife and son, both of whom spoke little French. Having unwittingly named his only friend 'Blockhead' in no way diminished Albert's love for the bird; he had taken to feeding Andouille from his hand and training the pigeon to return home. Anyone foolish enough to point out that passenger pigeons, unlike carrier pigeons, were not known for their homing instincts would have been silenced by the reproof of Andouille's unfailing constancy.

It is said that animals — birds in particular — are incapable of love. Still, something akin to that emotion must have flickered somewhere in Andouille's tiny heart or pea-sized brain, for he never allowed himself to be separated from Albert, seeking out the boy wherever he went as if the two were connected by an invisible line.

When Albert raised objections to his father's plans for him, specifically that he had never set foot in France and, being only sixteen years of age, was too young to join the army, M. Boucher waved his hands. "You're a strapping young man," he said, "and will easily pass for eighteen." He sat down on a log near the boy and lit his pipe. "As for the other, well, what of it? France is in our blood, eh, our hearts." He thumped his chest to indicate the place one can only assume this shrunken organ was perfunctorily hammering away and exhaled a long plume of blue smoke. "'The War to End All Wars', they're calling it now. Wouldn't want to miss out on that, eh? Might not get another chance."

"Will you be coming, too?" Albert asked, having clearly missed the entire drift of his father's words.

M. Boucher sighed, releasing another cloud of smoke. "Would that I could," he said. "Nothing would give me greater joy than to drive *les Boches* back across the Rhine and right up the Kaiser's *derrière*." He smiled as though imagining the scene. "Alas, I am too old now. This is sport for youth."

Albert, seeing that his father's mind was set, and without other recourse, eventually agreed that he would go. The boy knew nothing of war and little of anything else in the world, so he was not as frightened as perhaps he should have been. He raised his arm, and Andouille flapped down to perch on it. "Perhaps I shall learn to fly, too," Albert said. He had never spoken this dream aloud before, for his dreams were few and precious. "Shall I bring Andouille along with me?" he asked. "I suspect he would like an adventure."

"Of course, of course," said M. Boucher. "The French know exactly what to make of a squab."

So, the matter decided, Albert stowed his few belongings in a small satchel and Andouille in a cage he had woven out of willow branches. Judit hugged Albert and told him to be good. M. Boucher clapped his son on the shoulder. *"Vive la liberté,"* he said, handing the boy a scrawled note fraudulently attesting that Albert had just turned eighteen. "What a time you will have, no?" Then he took Judit by the arm and led her back towards their cabin.

Albert journeyed by barge down the Nelson River to Warren Landing and then onto a steamer that travelled the length of Lake Winnipeg. The boat was crowded with men and boys who, like Albert, had travelled from nameless places along nameless waters, drawn like metal filings to some great invisible magnet. The nights aboard were loud and filled with strange accents, coarse laughter, and drunken brawls. Some of the men teased Albert, pointing to Andouille's cage, grinning and rubbing their stomachs.

Albert had little trouble finding the recruitment office in Winnipeg: a long line of men of all ages and walks of life stretched down Main Street for nearly half a block. Out-of-work voyageurs in buckskin stood shoulder to shoulder with well-dressed college boys while a group of Red Cross volunteers moved down the line, handing out sandwiches wrapped in cloth. A young woman with dark hair handed one to Albert. "Hello," she said, "I am Aimée" She knelt to peer into Andouille's cage. "And who is this?"

"Andouille," Albert said.

Aimée stood, laughing, and brushed dust from her white skirt. "That is a terrible name," she said. Then her smile faded as she looked into Albert's eyes. "Go home," she said, instinctively reaching to clutch a small gold ring fastened around her throat with a delicate chain. "It is very bad over there." She brushed a tangled lock of hair away from Albert's eyes. "Be brave," she said. "Take your little bird and run away."

"My papa says I must fight for France."

Aimée spat into the dust. "Tell them that you are a cook, then," she said, pointing towards the recruiting office.

"I fear they will eat Andouille in France."

"No," Aimée said. "It is a grave crime to harm a pigeon. All the generals agree."

M. Boucher need not have feared that Albert's youth would deny him the opportunity for glory in battle: no one in the recruitment office bothered to ask Albert how old he was, and, by some strange turning of fate, Albert and Andouille were spared the muddy butchery of the trenches and given instead a privilege normally reserved for the sons of the wealthy and high-born: the terrible beauties of the sky. There, high above the bloody fields of France, talents that the schools in Paris and London would never deign to refine in this poor woodcutter's son would be burnished in service of the Royal Flying Corps.

Early in the summer of 1916, Albert and Andouille arrived at the RFC aerodrome in St Omer. Albert, with the rank and uniform of Air Cadet and a salary of $1.10 per day — and Andouille, with no official rank, and rations of seed and corn as payment — were assigned to the observer corps. Albert quickly demonstrated an aptitude for sketching, photography, and the intricacies of the Hythe camera: a Lewis machine-gun frame fitted with a film canister instead of an ammunition drum.

Despite his obvious utility as a messenger, Andouille caused no end of trouble for the handlers by refusing to remain in the mobile loft to which he had been assigned. Each night he would escape and seek out Albert in his barracks, tapping at the glass with his beak and cooing mournfully until someone opened the window. This nocturnal ritual earned Albert the nickname 'Heathcliff' from Captain Thomas Yeats, who commanded the squadron. "If I wanted to sleep in a stinking room filled with feathers and pigeon shit," Yeats said, "I would have stayed in Belfast."

Still, despite his complaints, Yeats was fond of Albert, and when the pigeon handlers came to retrieve Andouille, Yeats informed them that the bird had been reassigned to No. 2 Squadron and promoted to the rank of major. "Any future communications with our new officer must come through the appropriate channels," Yeats told them, "and with the proper paperwork."

When Albert thanked him, Yeats said, "By Christ, we'd all be better off with the bird in charge." Having spent the first years of the war in the infantry with the Inniskilling Fusiliers, Yeats had little faith in his superiors. Instead of sending him home when his left leg had been shattered at the Battle of Loos, the Brass Hats had reassigned him to the Royal Flying Corps where it was thought that his inability to walk without the use of a cane would prove no hindrance in a cockpit.

Albert was overjoyed when he was assigned to Yeats's plane. Though he would never speak the words aloud, in his heart he loved the young captain. He would love him forever, and in the silence of that moment, he vowed that he would walk through fire for him.

The morning of their first patrol, Yeats found Albert waiting beside their new R.E. 8, the boy's flight suit hanging from his thin frame like a poorly-pitched tent, a mobile roost —from which Andouille's head protruded—tucked under his arm. The bird rotated his neck to gawk at Yeats with one wide, insipid eye.

Yeats shook his head. "Both of you keep your bleedin' heads down," he said, "and do exactly as I say."

"Yes, sir," Albert said, patting Andouille's head. "We're ready to do our duty."

Yeats withdrew a flask from a pocket in his flight jacket and took a swig. "My da told me I'd die fightin' against the Brits or for them," he said.

Albert, whose knowledge of world events was on par with Andouille's, did not quite grasp the meaning of Yeats's words. "So you chose to fight for them?"

"Pay's better," Yeats said. "Apart from that, they can all kiss my arse." He clambered up into the forward cockpit, wincing as he hauled his useless leg over the side, and said, "Now you and your eejit bird get up in this crate and try not to do anything foolish like gettin' yourselves killed."

Their first mission was to photograph German positions between Arras and Cambrai ahead of an imminent offensive: troops were massing in the trenches, and the British guns were raining shells on the German lines, sending up huge geysers of smoke and mud. Even at 3,000 feet, and over the roar of the plane's engine, Albert could hear their thunder.

The AA fire intensified as they banked wide and crossed over no-man's-land. Beneath them, a company of Royal Fusiliers was being butchered. A British artillery battery was firing short, and high-explosive shells were dropping among the stalled ranks, trapping the Fusiliers between the enemy machine guns and the creeping hail of deadly fire from their own field ordnance.

Albert hastily scrawled a note on a small slip of paper: "32 Brigade: check your fire!" He pulled Andouille from his carrier, and, with trembling hands, stuffed the message into the canister on the bird's leg. He leaned over the side of the cockpit and released Andouille into the slipstream. "Godspeed," he said as the pigeon flapped erratically back towards the British lines through clouds of smoke and shards of flak until he disappeared from Albert's sight.

That night, a battered corporal visited No. 2 Squadron's barracks on behalf of the remaining soldiers of Royal Fusilier Company C. The corporal handed a bottle of Old Orkney to Yeats and two bags of corn to Albert. "We thought we was done for," he said, gently stroking Andouille's head with a mud-stained hand. Then he stood at attention, saluted the bird, and walked back into the night.

Over the next several months, a kind of myth was woven around Captain Yeats's R.E. 8 and its strange crew. Soldiers who spotted the plane from the trenches saw it as a good omen — cheered, perhaps, by the thought that someone was watching over them from above, ready to send out a tattered emissary to aid them when all seemed lost.

One bitter day in late November 1917, the legend came to an end. Yeats and Albert were patrolling near Cambrai, escorted by two Nieuport fighters. Their mission was to report back on the advance of 300 British tanks assaulting the Hindenburg Line. Heavy cloud cover forced Yeats to fly low over the battlefield, and Albert was awestruck by the smoke-belching behemoths crawling across the muddy fields, impervious to anything but a direct hit from an enemy shell.

From the left flank, through plumes of fire and fog, Albert saw horses racing past the rumbling tanks and speeding towards the enemy lines. Albert cried out and pointed, for the cavalry charge was the most beautiful thing he had yet witnessed. And the most terrible: elemental creatures of flesh and muscle and sinew, born to run, unleashed to race headlong into a wall of steel and bullets and death.

It was later reported that a squadron of Fort Garry horsemen had not received the orders to stand down and allow the tanks to break through. Now they were charging, bright swords glinting in the muted sunlight, straight into the German guns. The horses flew across the broken land, muscles rippling as they ran. Behind them, the slow onslaught of tanks. Before them, rank upon rank of enemy machine guns. Albert watched in horror as the horses and riders began to fall under the withering fire. Still they charged, undaunted.

Yeats banked the plane to follow their progress, and he and Albert witnessed a wonder: battle-grim German soldiers with their mechanized killing machines, perhaps awed by the sight of all the heroes from their glorious boyhood stories galloping towards them, stood and raised their hands in surrender. Albert shouted as the cavalry smashed through the lines, sabres flashing, and raced on.

Then, because this was the twentieth century and chivalry was long dead, the German soldiers returned to their guns, firing into the ranks of horsemen as they rode past.

The charge ended abruptly some 250 yards beyond the German gun positions, checked by a sheer drop into a swift, muddy river. The horsemen flung themselves to the ground and took shelter in the ravine. The horses fled, riderless and terrified, back across the battlefield.

Seeing the plight of the cavalry soldiers, Yeats signalled his wingmen to attack the enemy gunners. Perhaps Yeats, too, was moved by the romantic charge of the Fort Garry horsemen, for he slammed the stick forward, dove after the Nieuports, and began strafing the enemy positions. As they banked around to make a second pass, one of the Nieuports beside them erupted in flames, the pilot fighting for control for several seconds before his plane slammed into the ground and exploded.

Tracer bullets whizzed past their plane. Albert swivelled around and saw a trio of Albatros biplanes lining up behind them. Moments later, the second escort fighter was shot to ribbons and sent tumbling from the sky. Yeats broke away, but the old R.E. 8 was no match for the swift German fighters, and he could do no more than curse as a hail of bullets ripped through the cowling of their plane. Dark black smoke poured out of the engine as it died.

Yeats, blinded by oil, banked hard to reach the British lines, but the forward struts had been shot away, and their crate began to come apart in the air. The engine burst into flames as they skidded over the ground, coming to a halt some fifty yards from where the Fort Garry horsemen were pinned down.

Albert threw Andouille's carrier over the side and leaped down. He turned back to the plane and saw Yeats slumped over the control column, flames creeping towards the cockpit. His first reaction was to run from the wreckage, but something called him back. He clambered onto the wing and reached through the searing heat to unlatch Yeats's seat belt and pull him out of the aircraft.

It was not until much later that Albert realized how badly his hands were burned. At this moment, his only thought was the open expanse of churned-up earth that lay between them and the temporary safety of the ravine. He crouched down by Andouille's cage and set the bird free. "Live," he said, as Andouille flapped away through skies filled with lead and smoke. Albert grabbed onto Yeats's flight jacket with one hand and began stumbling across the muddy ground, dragging the unconscious pilot behind him. He could hear the horsemen ahead of him shouting encouragement. Two of the men tried to come to his aid but were cut down by the German guns. Only faith in miracles could explain how Albert managed to reach the ravine through that ceaseless storm of bullets.

"Brave lad," said a young lieutenant when Albert finally dropped down over the embankment and a medic had been summoned to see to Yeats. "But I fear you're out of the frying pan and into the fire. We are well and truly cooked here."

It was true. Even as he spoke, German trench mortars were zeroing in on the trapped Fort Garry horsemen. Shells rained down among the cowering men, and the air was filled with the smell of high explosive, shards of steel, and the heart-rending cries of wounded men and dying horses. Albert ran to Yeats, who was slipping in and out of consciousness, and knelt beside him. Yeats looked up. "Guess my da was right," he said.

Albert raised his eyes, expecting to meet his death. Instead, from out of the fire and smoke, he saw a bird descending. It darted back and forth across the sky until it came to rest on his shoulder.

Andouille's breast was covered in blood, but Albert could not find the wound. He looked around at the dying soldiers and then back to Andouille. "I'm sorry," he said as he scribbled down a message: "Garry Horse trapped behind lines: Meuse Wood." He released Andouille back into the maelstrom. Albert watched as the bird flapped away over the enemy lines. Andouille was nearly across when a shotgun blast erupted from one of the craters and swatted him from the sky.

Heedlessly, Albert cried out and climbed over the lip of the ravine. A nearby horseman grabbed him, but Albert wrestled himself free and began to run towards the place where Andouille had fallen. As the pitiless bullets tore through him, Albert felt certain that he saw his mother's face (God rest her soul) smiling down on him. Had he hesitated a moment longer, he might have caught a glimpse of Andouille rising again from the blood-soaked mud.

Late in the fall of 1919, M. Boucher was chopping wood when he looked up and saw four horsemen riding towards his cabin. He found himself trying to remember the last time he'd spoken to another human being. The years since his son's departure had been hard ones: Judit returned to live with her mother in Winnipeg, and an improperly set fracture left M. Boucher with a permanent limp and constant pain.

He put down his axe and wiped his brow, watching as the riders neared. Two wore cavalry uniforms; the others were dressed in civilian clothes. One carried a birdcage beside him on the saddle. M. Boucher's heart raced.

The two civilians dismounted, and one of them took a cane from the saddle and limped towards the house. As he neared, M. Boucher could see that the left side of the man's face was covered in thick scars and one ear was burned away. Albert walked behind him, carrying a cage. "I'm Thomas Yeats," the burned man said. "Your son is home."

The two Fort Garry horsemen departed the next day, but Yeats remained for a week. Albert begged him to stay, but Yeats was determined to return to Ireland, where another war was brewing. "I'll come back," he said, "once my countrymen finally decide there's been enough killing."

In the ensuing days, M. Boucher learned what had befallen Albert and Andouille since he'd sent them from Norway House, of how Albert was shot and Andouille saved an entire squadron of cavalry from certain doom. Though broken and bleeding, Andouille had delivered the message, and three tanks were diverted to rescue the trapped Fort Garry horsemen. Albert was shot through the neck and could now speak only in a hoarse whisper. Andouille, despite having received the best veterinary attention available, would never fly again.

"They have come through hell to be here," Yeats said.

Years of regret and folly had accumulated on M. Boucher's thick skull, bowing him until he had ceased to even dream that anything he had once cared for might return to him. "My son," he said, "I am cursed forever for sending you away."

Andouille died peacefully one afternoon in early spring, as the setting sun turned the Nelson River to molten gold and gulls wheeled and screeched over the docks where fishermen were unloading the day's catch. Albert found his companion perched upon a rafter in the woodshed as though asleep. "Godspeed," he said. Then he left the shed and stood in the yard, watching the world diminish into darkness, sending out whatever unseen signal had summoned the bird to him in days past, a silent call that could conjure bright spirits from far away.

When no answering cry came, Albert returned to the woodshed and lit a single lamp. Then, taking up his notebook, he sat long into the night, sketching flying machines in cloudless skies and birds in flight.

THE RAVEN SHORT STORY CONTEST

© 2023, Cate Sandilands, Alison Stevenson

THE 2022 RAVEN SHORT STORY CONTEST

You heard the call and flocked to the 2022 Raven Short Story Contest. Thank you to all submitting authors for sharing your wonderful stories and supporting Pulp Literature Press. From so many gems, our wonderful Leo X Robertson collected the shiniest stories and decided which truly gleamed. In his words: *This was a great experience for me — apart from having to pick one top story above the others. When it comes to further narrowing down a Pulp competition shortlist, it really is splitting hairs. I hope all writers who made it to this top spot know that they absolutely nailed it and made this job very difficult!*

FIRST PLACE: 'Revolutions' by Cate Sandilands
Exquisite descriptions transport the reader. This piece so well encapsulates that post-university time in life when you're brimming with desire to change the world without having many tools to do so. Beautiful, melancholy, highly recommended.

FIRST RUNNER-UP: 'Foam' by Alison Stevenson
A lovely elegiac piece about how human it is to fail, how brave it is to accept that — and how frustrating it is that you have to. I really felt for the protagonist, perhaps because of his flaws. That's tough for a writer to achieve.

SECOND RUNNER-UP: 'All Our Swains Commend Her' by Mitchell Toews
What I thought the most while reading this one for the first time was: 'This must have taken so long to write!' Every sentence is packed with detail and not

a word is spared. A highly skilled piece of writing with a lot to say about the way we live and how we treat one another. Can't believe such a short piece of writing left me with such memorable characters and so much to think about!

HONOURABLE MENTION: 'Marty' by Kevin Sandefur
The more I read this story, the bigger my grin was—as I assume was its intended impact! A fur-filled delight. I would love to have a cat like Marty in my back garden and annoy my partner with how much love and attention I give him!

THE 2022 RAVEN SHORTLIST

'God in Tokyo' by Finnian Burnett
'Marty' by Kevin Sandefur
'Revolutions' by Cate Sandilands
'Choose Any Dream' by Florence Rose Scollard
'Foam' by Alison Stevenson
'Rules of Engagement' by Charity Tahmaseb
'All Our Swains Commend Her' by Mitchell Toews
'Yakety Hex' by KT Wagner

Cate Sandilands *is a professor of Environmental Arts and Justice in the Faculty of Environmental and Urban Change at York University, and a graduate of the Writer's Studio at Simon Fraser University. Her most recent book is the edited creative collection* Rising Tides: Reflections for Climate Changing Times *(Caitlin, 2019). Both her academic and creative writing can be found on her website, catesandilands.ca. Her story 'Anna, Knitting' was recently shortlisted for the Peter Hinchcliffe Short Fiction Award and will be published in* The New Quarterly *in Spring, 2023.*

ℛEVOLUTIONS

BY CATE SANDILANDS

It's a hot August day—hot, at least, for Vancouver Island—and I'm in the middle of the bench front seat of an old Ford pickup, speeding along Highway 4 somewhere between Port Alberni and the T-junction at the coast that takes you to Ucluelet if you turn left or Tofino if you turn right. We've already passed through Cathedral Grove, where I wanted to stop because I loved going there with my parents when I was a kid. I remember the feeling of the huge trees with their thick, deeply-grooved bark and how small and protected I felt among them. The truck broke down in Nanaimo, though, so we're late, and we haven't even stopped to pee since we left the garage. The conversation has dwindled to silence, and the scenery has devolved into a monotony of scraggly, badly replanted clear-cuts. MacMillan Bloedel has announced these new stands with bright yellow-and-green signs. They're dated: 1968, 1972, 1979. The area around last year's sign, 1984, still looks like a dead zone.

I'm terrified, but I'm trying hard not to show it. It wouldn't be part of my newly cool political persona to say I'm afraid because I have no seatbelt, or because there's a steep drop down a cliff from the two-lane highway, or because Dan, who's driving because it's his truck and it can fit all our camping gear, is losing his vision and angry about it most of the time, or because he's holding on to the steering wheel with his left hand while he rolls a smoke in his right.

Dan's handmade Drum cigarettes are always perfect cylinders. Mine look like pathetic joints. Dan is older than the rest of us. He's the sort of man for whom physical competence is essential, even though he is, like the rest of us, a new BA graduate from the Sociology department, used to chasing theories and concepts rather than timber or coal or, as he did in his past life, fish. I admire his dexterity even as I close my eyes and clench my teeth when he veers the truck too close to the edge of the road.

On my right, in the shotgun seat, is Geoff, and I try not to hold his hand too tightly as we mount Sutton Pass and wind down the difficult road to the ocean. Geoff has decided I'm his girlfriend this summer, and I'm enjoying it. Geoff and his friends, including Dan, are Marxists. Several nights a week, they debate the finer points of socialist strategy over beers in the basement of the Student Union Building until it closes. Some of their passionate discussions seem silly to me — does it really matter whether the revolution arises from party politics or the workers' movement?—but I know better than to argue. I've never been part of a clique before, and I don't want to mess it up. Honestly, I'm not sure if I'm in love with Geoff or with the passage he grants me into his friends' intoxicating pool of bubbling, radical energy.

At this moment, I don't care about my motivations. I'm with Geoff, I'm going camping, and I'm part of the revolution. It's our last trip together before we all go in our different directions: me to graduate school at Queen's, Geoff to York, Dan to a quick BEd and teaching high school. I want to make the best of it. I stare straight ahead and focus on the shorter-term goal of getting to where we're going: the beach.

When the highway starts to flatten out, I loosen my grip on Geoff's hand just enough for him to feel I'm cool with the way things are going—but not so much that he'll forget I want to share every moment of our connection on this trip. I look over at him and see his wire aviator glasses have slipped down his nose and he's holding tightly to the hand rest on the truck door. I'm not sure what to do with the information that he's been afraid, too, this whole time. I reach over with my free hand, push his glasses up his nose, and smile. His grin back crystallizes the moment: yes, we're together.

At the T-junction, Dan turns right toward the national park and Schooner Cove, the only place we can officially camp on the beach. Dan told us there are squatters on some of the beaches outside the park, and also Native communities we should avoid so as not to piss them off by trespassing. That one beery conversation at the SUB was actually interesting: are parks part of the revolution or a tool of the bourgeoisie? Wasn't all that parkland stolen from Native people by the government in the first place? We agreed, in any case, to take a legal campsite rather than squat. Dan rolls another cigarette, Geoff squeezes my hand, and they start to talk about the quality of the block of hash Geoff has hidden inside his bedroll.

When we arrive at the Schooner Cove parking lot, I see Lucas's red Toyota, easily recognizable from the *Eat the Rich* and *Solidarność* bumper stickers. He and Sunita must already be on the beach, and they've probably been there for hours. We unpack the truck and distribute the load — equally, of course — and start the hike down the trail. The cedars along the way are even bigger than the firs I remember from Cathedral Grove, and I want to stop and touch them, to remember. But Geoff and Dan are determined to get to the campsite, so instead I readjust my pack, get a better grip on the box of food I've been allotted to carry because Geoff has his guitar, and try not to slow down to marvel at the massive presences of all those trees.

Way down at the far end of the beach, Lucas and Sunita have already set up their tent, hung up their food bag in a tree a short distance away, and lit a fire. Beside the fire, there's a neat pile of foraged firewood and a pot of steaming water on a flat rock. The campsite is encircled by large beached logs, and Lucas is sitting on one of them, alternately picking at the label of a Labatt 50 and poking the flames. Sunita is beside him, reading. She's always reading — she's smarter than the rest of us put together — and I sneak a peek at the title to make sure it goes on my reading list, too: *Pablo Neruda: Selected Poems, Bilingual Edition.* My heart sinks at the thought she's learning Spanish on top of everything else. They both get up. Sunita hugs me, says she's so glad I'm here. My spirits pick up again.

Geoff, Dan, and I deposit our gear on the sand and begin to set up. Dan raises his ancient canvas tent in no time and comes over to help Geoff and me with our nylon one. When both tents are finished, they look like a military fortress next to a neon-orange child's toy. I rummage through the food box for bread and cheese — we also haven't eaten since Nanaimo — and Geoff goes off to put the beer in the ocean to cool. When he comes back, I hand Dan and Geoff their sandwiches and, with my own, sit down on a nearby rock, looking out to the ocean. The surf is so loud I can only just hear the conversation on the other side of the fire, but I'm not really interested anyway. I breathe the salt air deeply, listen to the rhythmic pounding of sea on sand, and watch the clouds scud across the brilliant blue sky. If this is life after the revolution, I'm in.

My meditation is interrupted by shouting and whistling. I turn around and see Geoff and Lucas waving at two people up the beach, calling them over. When they get closer, I see the people are Joy and Christie, two women I know vaguely from our statistics class last term. They drop their tents on the far side of the campsite and join the circle. Apparently, Lucas ran into Joy at the library last week and invited her along, and she decided to bring Christie, too. The invitation confuses me — neither of them seems exactly revolutionary intellectual material, to put it mildly — but there they are, feathered bangs and all. I look over at Sunita and she shrugs. At least they brought food and two boxes of wine.

As the sun moves down the sky, Christie helps Sunita and me prepare the meal. She may not be an A student, but it turns out she has lots of camping experience and has thought to come with pre-chopped vegetables and bouillon cubes, which she throws in a pot with some red lentils and water to simmer on the fire. I'm impressed. Joy, on the other hand, starts in on the wine and turns giggly very quickly. Unlike in stats class, she's clearly done the math in terms of couples and is not very subtly flirting with Dan. I can't help but feel a smirk of satisfaction when he pulls a Swiss Army knife out of his shirt pocket and focuses intently on carving a piece of driftwood, obviously uninterested in whatever it is she's bubbling at him. As we slice tomatoes and cucumbers for a salad, Sunita teaches me a new word: *schadenfreude*.

By the time we've eaten and Christie, Sunita, and I have cleaned up — my evil eye at Geoff to come and help made no difference — the sun has almost set. I'm not sure I've ever seen anything so beautiful: the bands of pink and orange across the sky, pressed down further and further by the force of the inky blue and black; the unthinkably huge, fierce mass descending gracefully into the sea toward extinguishment. I sit with my beer and watch it disappear. As its afterglow fades, the stars start to show themselves. Unlike in the city, there are millions of them. I'm excited when I see one spark across the sky, then another, then another. Christie says the shooting stars are part of the Perseid meteor shower. I'm impressed again: I've underestimated her.

Geoff brings out his guitar and plays a few recognizable Dylan chords, but nobody else joins in. I sit down beside him and put my hand on his knee; he's absorbed in the instrument and doesn't respond, but I leave my hand there anyway. When the soapstone hash pipe makes its way around the circle to me, I inhale deeply before re-lighting it and holding it out to Geoff. As the pipe passes two, then three, then four times, I realize the music isn't coming from his guitar any more. It's coming from the meteors strumming the night sky. I let the vibrations slide into my ears and ripple down my torso and legs, out through my feet into the sand. I feel a low hum begin in the middle of my chest. It blooms up and outward, joining me to the chorus of water and forest now invisible in the darkness. I'm home. I feel my breath rise to a long, clear note, sustained and confident amid the elemental counterpoint.

As I open my mouth to release the note back to the stars, Lucas's voice tears through the music and severs my connection. It takes me a second to focus on what he's saying. It turns out he's expounding on the passage from Marx about life in a socialist utopia: hunting in the morning, fishing in the afternoon, rearing cattle in the evening, criticizing after dinner. Maybe it's the hash, and maybe it's because I can still feel the longing tingle of the meteoric dancing, but after a minute I find myself interrupting him. I ask, in a voice that doesn't quite feel like my own, who's going to make the meals and wash the dishes and look after the children and take care of the sick people. What will the deer and the fish and the cows think about this utopia? After dinner, will anyone be listening to the trees?

There's stunned silence for a minute before Geoff starts playing again, as if nothing at all has happened. Joy wobbles over, sits next to Geoff on the other side, and requests 'Hey Jude'. He hates The Beatles, so I'm surprised he knows all the words. Joy knows all the words too, it seems. Sunita gives me a long look. Christie makes a show of cringing at Joy's off-key *na na nas*. Her smile at me across the fire is conspiratorial.

Later, when I wake in the middle of the night and find that Geoff is no longer in our shared tent, I'm less disappointed than I think I should be. I lie in my sleeping bag, listening to the surf and the trees and the stars overhead singing among the meteors'

Perseid dances. I think about Christie and wonder if she's asleep yet. I think about the fact I'll be leaving for Kingston in a week but that the trees and the ocean will still be here when I return even if Geoff and the others won't. I imagine the sun rising somewhere over Lake Ontario on its circle back to the Pacific, to this place that so clearly calls me. And I understand, for the first time, that some revolutions may be about turning things around, but others involve coming back, again and again.

PULP Literature

Four awards for genre-busting fiction and poetry

The Bumblebee Flash Fiction Contest

Deadline: 15 February

Prize: $300

The Magpie Award for Poetry

Deadline: 15 April
First Prize: $500

The Hummingbird Flash Fiction Prize

Deadline: 15 June
Prize: $300

The Raven Short Story Contest

Deadline: 15 October
Prize: $300

For more information visit: pulpliterature.com/contests

Short stories, poetry, and comics you can't put down.

Alison Stevenson's work appears in PRISM international, The
New Quarterly, Prairie Fire, This Will Only Take a Minute:
100 Canadian Flash, *and* Three, Volume XX. *Her stories have
been finalists for the Alice Munro Festival Short Story Contest and
the Penguin Random House Student Fiction Award, and longlisted
for the CBC and TNQ/Peter Hinchcliffe prizes. Alison is working
on a story collection. Visit her at alisonstevensonwriter.com.*

FOAM

BY ALISON STEVENSON

Mark had been living at the Deerhorn Longstay Suites for a
month. His place included a kitchenette, a Formica table with
its fake wood-grain worn off in places, two dining chairs, and a
plaid sofa that smelled of upholstery cleaner. At least it was clean.
It was not the kind of accommodation he would have chosen
for a vacation or a business trip. But in the circumstances it had
seemed like the best option. And anyway, it was only temporary.

He'd never bring Alistair there—he'd wait until he had a
proper place. Or maybe there was still a chance it wouldn't come
to that. Instead, when it was his turn to have Alistair, they'd go
to the kinds of places an eight-year-old would want to go to: a

Jays game, the dinosaurs at the museum, an indoor skateboard park where, from a second-floor viewing area, Mark watched his son navigate various obstacles and inclines for an hour or so. Then Swiss Chalet for dinner before Mark dropped him back at home.

Hard to believe a month had passed since the call from Saundra telling him not to come back to the house when he got back from his business trip—that he should find somewhere else to stay. "I'm sure that won't be a problem for you."

Mark heard the air quotes around 'business trip'. He hadn't needed to ask what she was talking about. He thought about asking, but he'd played that card before. He didn't want to make her say it, and he didn't want to hear her say it again. "I'm sorry—"

"No, don't, just … don't."

After Saundra had hung up, Mark continued to stand with his phone pressed against his cheek. Across the hotel room—in a charming establishment in a picturesque town—Darlene was sitting on the bed switching between channels with the remote. Wrapped in a hotel bathrobe, dark wavy hair still wet from the shower, she looked younger than she was. He'd been spending so much time and energy arranging ways to be with her over the previous few months. Now he felt tired. He lowered the hand with the phone.

"Who was that?" she asked, without looking away from the TV screen. "Bad news?"

"It was nothing, just … work."

Over the remainder of the getaway with Darlene, things about her that had attracted him—her uninhibited laugh, her wiry energy, even the way she walked—began to strike Mark as tiresome. Once they got back to Toronto, he found he wasn't interested in seeing her again.

Saundra gave him a time she'd be out of the house so he could come by and pick up his things. He took just a few pieces of clothing and left everything else where it was. It didn't make sense to bring any belongings to the Deerhorn — such a stupid name; deer don't even *have* horns. He had no desire to feel at home there.

What Mark missed most were the casual, everyday moments with Alistair, those intimacies that couldn't be recreated on a part-time basis. He missed seeing him in his pyjamas. He missed Alistair leaning against him on the sofa, missed smelling the top of his head. It just wasn't the same doing it at the McDonald's. He'd known he would miss his son — of course he would; what kind of jerk wouldn't miss his own son? But Mark hadn't been prepared for the physical sense of loss. Worse was the distance he felt between himself and Alistair when he did see him, as though he was just a visitor in his son's life. He always came away feeling defeated, as if he could have done something to make everything okay if only he'd been able to figured out what.

On the way to the office, Mark picked up a coffee from the hipster pour-over coffee place on the corner. That was another thing he missed: the built-in espresso machine he and Saundra had installed as part of the kitchen reno. The large cube of brushed steel with chrome knobs and dials and nozzles cost more than his first car. He'd loved how it growled, the whooshing sounds, the steam. He wondered whether Saundra ever used it, or if she'd even learned how.

Mark had got his start in real-estate development when he was still in his twenties, back when he had that same first car.

He bought a dilapidated house, got some friends together to fix it up, and flipped it — long before everyone started doing the same thing. He grew the business gradually, never getting in over his head. And he'd been lucky.

As the business grew, Mark had always made sure he understood enough about the trades that he could form his own judgements. He always hired good people to work for him and paid them well. But recently he'd lost some of that direct involvement, maybe come to rely too much on the people running the various parts of the business. There hadn't been any problems but, without his noticing it, the company had become too big for him to have a view on everything that was going on. He'd lost sight of things. He really needed to get back to the principles that had made his company a success, immerse himself in the details he could control. Get his mind off the other things.

When he got to the office, he headed over to the rentals group. Linda had been with the company since nearly the beginning and had known him for years. It was comforting to see her at her desk like always. He asked her how things were going.

"The usual. I was just about to send someone out to check on some tenants in the Junction block. The cheque bounced and they're not answering calls or emails. Last month, they called in advance and asked for more time, and we gave it to them. This month they didn't ask."

"I could go," he said.

Mark never got involved at the level of dumpy little mom-and-pop storefronts, or delinquent tenants. He had people for that — not just Linda, but a whole department that dealt with the tenants of properties his acquisitions team bought as they assembled larger parcels for development.

"Really?" Linda regarded him quizzically.

"I spend too much time in the office working with numbers and lawyers," said Mark, knowing how odd he must be sounding. "I should get out more — you know, see what's going on in the real world once in a while."

Linda gave him the details and the key. She cast him a sceptical look as he left.

He pulled up outside the address. It was in a backwater section of the street, a few blocks outside the active business area and beyond reach of the bus route. The building had a restaurant on the first floor and an apartment above. The lights were off. It looked deserted. Through the window he could see there were no tables or chairs. He unlocked the door and went in.

He walked through the empty space to the kitchen at the back of the restaurant. It was almost bare. The tenants had taken most of the equipment. They'd left the place clean, he had to give them that. The kitchen equipment was theirs, of course, but if Mark's people had gotten there before the tenants skipped out, they would have seized it to pay the back rent. The miscellaneous dishes and utensils, the half-used bag of flour, and the other things that had been left behind would all go in the trash.

A rapping sound came from the front. He went out to see what it was. On the other side of the glass door, a man was holding a box, which he raised when he saw Mark.

Mark unlocked the door. "Andersons," the man said. "Bakery order. Short on almond croissants, so we substituted chocolate."

He glanced around the unlit restaurant and towards the counter. "Where're Terry and Anna?"

Where a large multi-cup espresso machine must once have stood, there was a stain on the wall. There were crumbs and coffee grounds on the counter and a copper pipe sticking up like a long, crooked finger.

"Gone," said Mark. "Skipped out."

"Really. That's a shame. Good people."

He paused a second — a moment of silence for the departed — then, gesturing with the box, said, "This is paid for — Andersons doesn't take credit. Or returns." He put the box down on the ledge beside him. "Enjoy."

After the man was gone, Mark went up the stairs to the apartment. Like the restaurant, it was mostly empty. Occupying much of the tiny living room was a hulking old sofa upholstered in scratchy blue. It had deco-looking carved wood on the fronts of the armrests, the varnish peeling. It was either trendy and ironic or tired and sad, depending on which way you looked at it. Was it a piece of junk, or something they'd only reluctantly jettisoned in their flight because it was too heavy to get down the stairs?

What had the bakery man called them? Terry and Anna? Mark tried to visualize them strategizing at the kitchen counter, trying to figure out how they could keep going, what they should do differently, how they might salvage the crumbs of their optimism. Mark was an entrepreneur himself, but he'd never understood these little service businesses operating on razor-thin margins, trading labour, worry and hope for the chance of a tiny subsistence. It was always a balancing game with the struggling small business tenants: between how long they could make a go of it before giving up on their dream, and how long Mark let them keep trying to turn things around.

Something was sticking up between the sofa cushions. Mark reached over and pulled it out—a plastic giraffe. Alistair had had one just the same when he was a baby; for a while it had been his favourite thing.

What would it be like to live here? The apartment itself was cramped, but the light was good. A coat of paint and a refresh of the floors would help a lot. Or, if you had both floors of the building, you could get rid of the kitchen upstairs and open up the space: two or three bedrooms and a bathroom upstairs; knock out the wall downstairs between the kitchen and the big restaurant space. There was probably brick behind the plaster walls. High ceilings. He could bring down the blue sofa, assuming the tenants never came back for it, and move in his sound system and the leather recliner that Saundra never liked. He and Alistair could sit on the blue sofa together.

He'd keep the counter the way it was, and get a big espresso machine like the tenants had had. Alistair would sit on a stool at the counter, just like he used to do on early weekend mornings before Saundra was awake, when Mark would act as Alistair's personal barista, saying, "One steamer coming right up. Here you go, sir," as he pushed a cup of steamed milk across the kitchen island toward his son.

And Alistair would laugh, and lean over the cup of steamed milk with its thick head of foam, and examine the stiff froth of milk bubbles, prodding it and carving it delicately with the back of his spoon. He would hum a tuneless tune as he guided the spoon through the drifts of white. And Mark, from the other side of the counter, would observe Alistair's half-closed eyelids fluttering as he surveyed the pristine foam-world. He could hear his son's breath, the way the air huffed out intensely through his nose, as it always did when he was engrossed in something.

For Alistair, Mark believed, the ability to turn liquid milk into a semi-solid was his father's superpower. Alistair knew nothing of his father's extensive business interests.

What about a coffee shop in the restaurant space? The blue sofa could be part of a seating area with an electric fireplace on the wall. The afternoon light would spill across the counter as the boy worked on his homework after school. Simple, friendly banter from the regulars, jazz playing on the sound system in the background. Maybe Saundra, coming in to pick up Alistair, would take in the cosy scene, smile at her son, and then look across at him and—

A noise from the first floor broke his reverie. "Hello?" a woman's voice called. Mark felt a lurch in this chest. He rushed down the stairs.

"Are you open?" The middle-aged woman gestured to the box on the ledge beside her, then looked over toward the counter. "All I want is a muffin and coffee."

"It's closed," he said, voice harsh with disappointment. She looked surprised at his tone, and hurt.

"Here," he added more gently, grabbing the pastry box and holding it out to her. "There's no coffee, but please have these."

When she was gone, he locked the door, then turned back to the restaurant space. It was almost like some part of him expected to see the bright café of his imagination. Instead, he faced a meagre, sordid, abandoned place, full of nothing but squandered hopes. He felt heavy, punctured, no longer able to fend off the truth.

He trudged back up the stairs and sat down on the sofa. The springs were shot. He ran one hand over the rough surface of the fabric, the loopy texture stiff against his fingertips. He loosened his grip on the plastic giraffe that was still in his other hand. He'd been holding himself up with childish daydreams and illusions as fleeting and insubstantial as bubbles. It was time to accept how things were and stop pretending the old life was still there waiting for him to come back. He'd need to start looking for an apartment—something more permanent than the place he had, somewhere Alistair could visit.

He hadn't been thinking clearly when he was falling over himself trying to be with Darlene. He hadn't been weighing all the stakes. He'd taken the important things for granted—he who had made a career of calculating risk and return, planning and strategizing before any demolition began. And now he'd torn down everything that meant anything without even thinking about it. If he was lucky, he might be able to build some kind of relationship with Alistair out of the fragile materials that were left.

Mark surveyed the cramped apartment, with its cracked walls, chipped paint. A musty smell. The place would most likely sit vacant until the whole block was torn down. Unlikely they'd get new tenants in the meantime; who would want to spend the effort building up goodwill for a business in a location that was obviously slated for the wrecking ball? A high-rise would take its place. There would be shiny new apartments, new lives built upon the rubble of the old.

Mark took out his cell and dialled the office. He told Linda to send the locksmith over to change the locks. He shoved the giraffe back between the cushions and heaved himself out of the sofa.

DRAGON'S GREED

Sherilyn Moreton & Anat Rabkin

Sherilyn has been telling stories since she was a child, and she dreams of walking through the back of a wardrobe and meeting a mystical lion in a magical land. When she is not reading or writing, she is painting D&D miniatures or crocheting. She currently lives in Vancouver, British Columbia.

Anat has been drawing since she was old enough to hold a pencil, and dreaming up stories even longer. She has been published in multiple issues of comic anthologies by Cloudscape Comics Society. Anat's previous Pulp Literature appearances include 'Forbidden Fruit' (Issue 9), 'It Rained Then Too' (Issue 13), and 'For the Love of Grey' (Issue 17).

© 2023, Sherilyn Moreton & Anat Rabkin

I LOVE HER.
SHE DOESN'T UNDERSTAND

MAKE ME A MAN SO
THAT I MAY LOVE HER.
GIVE ME THE
OPPORTUNITY TO
BE ONE WHO LOVES
HER MOST OF ALL

MAKE ME ABLE TO BE NEAR HER AT ALL TIMES,
SO THAT I MIGHT LOVE HER MOST OF ALL.
LET ME FORGET IT ALL.
LET HER BE HAPPY.
LET HER BE WHOLE.
DISCARD ME.

...LET ME BE WHATEVER SHE NEEDS.
Dragon's Greed

THE SHEPHERDESS: THE TRAIL OF YELLOW ROSES

JM Landels

Once a shepherdess, a lady's maid, and a physician's apprentice, Antoinette Berger now finds herself in a new role as an agent of the Silver Branch. Her first task is to travel from Paris to La Tectume, an ancient castle at the feet of the Pyrenees, with a message for her errant patron, Madame, the self-styled Countess of Athlone. With her, she has taken Luc, the Parisien flower seller who has become her valet; her adopted hound, Jacques; and Luc's donkey, Babette.

JM Landels *is torn between travelling the world to teach writing and swordfighting, and never leaving her idyllic farm in Langley, BC. Her debut series, fantasy bestseller* Allaigna's Song: Overture, *and the sequels,* Aria *and* Chorale, *are available from Pulp Literature Press and Amazon. You can follow her adventures with pen and sword at jmlandels.stiffbunnies.com.*

© 2023, JM Landels

The Shepherdess: The Trail of Yellow Roses

The funds Grandmère Paris and the Duchesse d'Orléans had vouchsafed me were perilously low by the time Luc and I spotted the tumbledown walls of La Tectume. From the road far down in the valley, the partially ruined *château fort* was barely distinguishable from the jagged rocks it perched upon. One more night in a roadside inn before we had to begin that withering climb.

There was a single pistole and a few deniers in my purse. Once we reached the château we would find refuge, I had been told, but whether it would come without a price I didn't know. Nonetheless, we couldn't tackle that steep road without a night's sleep, a meal, and some hay for Luc's donkey, Babette. Her milk had kept us from going hungry more than once on this exhausting journey, but her hips were showing more prominently, and the roll of fat on her neck had disappeared. A sheep will stop giving milk when she runs out of fat, and Babette's udder was smaller even than a ewe's right now.

It took the remainder of the afternoon to find an inn, for this was not the main road south to Spain. On our route from Paris, we had taken neither the westerly roads through Toulouse nor the easterly to Montpellier, but instead had walked due south, through tiny hameaux, farmlands, hills, and forests no doubt rife with wolves, bears, and criminals. Fortunately, Jacques and Babette were our guardians, and no marauder, animal or human, got past the double alarum of barking wolfhound and braying ass. It had been a long, slow journey that hardened our feet and our bodies, and an abandoned-looking inn was luxury enough for us.

There were no other animals in the yard when we led Babette in, and no smoke came from the chimney. Nonetheless, a dog barked when we knocked, which set off Jacques as well. At last, a narrow man, bent nearly double with age, opened the door, spat in the dirt that served as a lintel, and asked, "What?"

"My brother and I seek a room for the night, good sir."

He looked me up and down with rheumy eyes, then said in a southern accent so filled with extra syllables I could barely parse it, "Two pistolas each-a one-a."

It was far more than we had, and an outrageous sum for what could surely be no more than basic board. Still, best not to antagonize the only innkeeper around. I gave a curtsy better fit for the court of Versailles, than for a dirty stoop in a forgotten corner of the country.

"Good sir, that is beyond our means." I carefully pronounced each 'e' I would normally leave silent. "But we can offer you ass's milk," I said, hoping Babette was not quite dry, "and I can read your palm and tell your future in the cards." The latter was a gamble, for we had been run out of town for making such offers before.

He spat another streak of dark saliva onto the dirt at our feet. "What do I need with my future told? Can't you see there's hardly any left? And I don't want milk from your scrawny ass. But …"

He grinned, showing a crenellated mouth of stained and crooked teeth. "I'll gladly see what your paps hold, sweet thing. Your brother can sleep in the stable, and you can warm my bed. No charge."

I put a hand on Luc's elbow to restrain him. Navigating the land with him had meant far fewer of these offers than I would otherwise expect, but there were still those who had nothing to lose.

"We'll both sleep in your stable, good sir, and we'll give you two sous for some bread and some hay, if you have it." Unless this scrawny rooster had a stout wife or sons nearby, there was no way he could prevent us from sleeping there. I had little hope he'd share any bread he might have, but a glance into the meagre shelter that served as a stable showed a pile of hay that seemed moderately dry and green.

He whistled through his gap teeth and a hound nearly as old as her master came limping up, wrinkling her nose and grumbling. Jacques, who had been busy watering all the corners of the barren frontage, rushed back to my side and stood at attention, hackles raised.

The old bitch wagged her tail, sneezed, and rushed out to greet the newcomers, wriggling like a puppy. No threat there.

I curtsied again. "Thank you for your hospitality, sir," I said, and led Luc by his rigid elbow to the stable.

"Let me hit him. Just once," he seethed at me.

"And what good would that do? It certainly wouldn't get us bread, unless we robbed his cupboard, which is almost certainly bare. We are not thieves, Luc." Or at least I wasn't, I thought, remembering Luc's adventure in the orangerie at the Luxembourg gardens. "We'll be just as comfortable in the stable, and there will be fewer fleas."

The latter was probably true, though the former proved not to be.

After a meagre meal consisting of the hard end of a sausage and an even harder heel of sweaty cheese that had been with us since Narbonne, we made our bed in the haystack, away from the side on which Babette was happily foraging.

We slept back to back, one blanket beneath us and two on top, as we had for most of the journey. I was used to sleeping with a gaggle of sisters and brother, but it had taken Luc most of the journey to stop spending the first third of every night twitching and shifting. Tonight he was back to his original innervated self.

"Luc, be still," I hissed finally, when the moon had crossed over the roof beam and begun shining in the window of the barn.

"I cannot sleep," he declared. "Something is just not right here. I feel trouble in the air."

"Well, trouble is best faced on a full stomach and a good night's sleep, so if we cannot have one, we should at least attempt the other."

"You sleep," he declared. "I will stretch my legs."

"Just don't wake me when you come back," I said, rolling over and bundling all the blankets around me.

It seemed trouble arrived before I'd been asleep more than a few moments. I was prodded awake by the cold muzzle of an arquebus. *Where is Jacques?* was my first thought. *And Luc?* was my second.

From the stable yard beyond the shelter came the sound of milling horses, creaking carriage wheels, and shouts. That it had taken a prod to awaken me was testament to how tired I still was.

"Just a maid," called out the owner of the firearm. "And a donkey." To me, he said, "Up, girl. Are there any others?"

I shook my head. If they hadn't encountered Luc already, I saw no reason to suggest his presence. I stood, clutching the blankets around me not for warmth, but simply so as not to lose them. I wondered if these were brigands, and if the contents of our small cart were already taken. Babette, the traitor, had raised no alarm at all, her face still buried up to her bushy brows in the pile of hay.

"Bring her inside," said another voice, and M'sieur arquebus nudged me forward into the now-crowded stable yard. From the far side of the building, someone shouted, "Open up before I knock down this worm-eaten door!"

Monsieur Arquebus escorted me out of the yard and through the front door of the inn. "Light the fire, girl," he said.

I glanced at the gap-toothed landlord, wondering if he would mention I was no maid of his. But he was quivering like grass in a windstorm. It appeared as if no fire had been lit in months — a wonder with the *Cers* roaring through at this time of year.

"There is no wood, monsieur," I said in my best approximation of the deliberate southern voice.

"Then fetch dung from the stables. It can't smell any worse than it already does in here."

It was true. The air was fetid with the smell of things long dead. With little hope, I glanced again at the sickle-shaped landlord. He was dribbling like an infant and likely pissing his trews at the same time. I hurried outside, escaping the stench but running headlong into another man — one I recognized.

"Parrrdonnez-moi," I drawled, as I rebounded off the worn velvet of Sauvegarde's manteau.

Once safely in the shelter of the barn, I leaned against the wall, huffing and trembling as much as the landlord. What cursed luck could put Sauvegarde and me in the same inn — twice? And in opposite ends of the realm? He hadn't seemed to recognize me when I collided with him by the door. I considered hitching up Babette and leaving before he did. But what of Luc and Jacques? My eye drifted to the wrapped bundle in the cart, which contained the rapier we'd carried all the way from Paris.

I unwrapped a corner of the cloth—a panel of red-and-silver acanthus leaf brocade—just enough to reveal the hilt of the sword. It was ornate, the swirling guard detailed as if it were made of chain, each link in itself stamped with a tiny chain pattern. The pommel—a term I didn't know then, but have learned in the time since—was not solid but an almost complete circle, broken at the top and flared like horns. I had no idea how unusual such a design was, nor its significance. My concern was the blade. I flipped the cloth open some more, revealing specks of rust that had accumulated along the length of the steel during our long and often wet journey south. But I knew how sharp even a rusted pair of shears could be, and doubted the splotches of rust would hinder the steel on its way through flesh.

It was Sauvegarde's, and I had every wish to return it to him through his body.

But I couldn't walk back into the inn and challenge the man to a duel. I doubted I could even walk in and stab him in the back while making it out alive. The yard was still bustling with people—more than Sauvegarde's usual three cronies—unhitching and untacking horses. The sound of iron shoes clopped towards the stable, so I took the rapier from the cloth and thrust it deep into the back corner of the haystack, where even the greediest horse shouldn't find it .

"Girl," said a man leading horses in. "What are you doing here?"

"Fetching hay to burn, for there is no wood," I replied. I grabbed an armful of fodder, which Babette tried to steal back as I sidled between her and the cart. There was plenty of old dung, but it was horse's and ass's, not cowpats, which would have been better fuel. I threw handfuls of dried balls onto my armful of hay and headed back to the inn, still calculating my next move.

I kept my head down and hurried past the milling men inside, carrying my armload of hay and manure to the hearth. Someone had brought in a lanthorn from the carriage, which served only to illuminate the dusty despair of the room. As I laid out straw and dung in the cold and cobwebby hearth, Sauvegarde's loud voice carried over the clatter.

"You've got an hour, maybe two, to make yourselves comfortable. Eat, sleep, but be ready by the time the sky turns grey. And keep your belts done up. We've got but one lass to make us some victuals, and she won't have time to be greasing your posts."

As I stood, dusting my skirts off in front of the smoky fire, I kept my head down and my face turned away from his voice. Nonetheless, his hand found the back of my skirts and gave me a hearty slap.

"Food, lass — as much as you have. These men have been in the saddle all day, and you'd best fill their bellies before they fill yours."

The rapier danced before my vision. I recalled how, when Madame took it from Sauvegard so many months ago, she held it easily, as if she had been born to it. I cursed myself for not asking her or even Henri, damn his rotund corpse, to teach me.

"Si les souhaits étaient des chevaux, les mendiants monteraient," my mother used to say.

I made my way to the only other door in the room, guessing it must be the kitchen. I took the quivering landlord by the elbow and dragged him with me. "Come, Papa," I said in a loud voice. I noticed the one called Ètier on the other side of the room, cleaning the barrel of one of his pistols. I had no doubt that Sanglier and Louis-Auguste were here too, though I dared not lift my head to search them out.

"What food have you, old man?" I said after I had closed the door behind us. When he said nothing but continued to shake, I slapped his weathered face. "These are dangerous men," I hissed. "Feed them!"

"Nothing. I have nothing," he wailed. "Please …" He suddenly grew strength in his sickled back and bolted past me to another door. I hoped it was the scullery, but when he opened it, a cold night air burst in and doused the candle stub on the table.

I dashed after him, stumbling in the dark, but I managed to find the back of his collar and trap him at the threshold. Panic gave him the force of ten, but need did the same for me.

"Not so fast, M'sieur hare," I said.

In the moonlight slanting through the doorway, I caught the dim flash of the hatchet that had suddenly appeared in his hand. "You want to feed them?" he hissed. "Butcher that donkey!"

We wrestled over the axe. Youthful vigour won out, and I pulled it from his grasp.

"You can lick the cocks of those whoresons if you like," he spat. "I'm lighting a beacon." He headed away from the back door in a hobbling parody of a run.

I recalled the horrible moments when I was stuck in the carriage with Sauvegarde, the ornate-handled rapier — now buried in the hay — bruising my buttocks with every bound and jolt of the wheels; Ètier polishing his pistols as he was even now; the cold calculating stare of Louis-Auguste; the deadly ease with which Sanglier played with knives.

The temptation to bolt after the landlord was commanding—until I heard the report of an arquebus and a strangled scream. I shut the kitchen door and estimated the paces between myself and the rapier.

There was nothing in the cupboards save some wormy flour, a three-quarters-empty jar of shrivelled fêves, and some dusty barley. The cistern at the back of the kitchen was nearly empty as well, but I managed to pull up a measure of scummy water. No matter—I wasn't going to consume any of it. I threw the beans and barley into the cauldron and added a half bottle of vinegared wine, hoping its dark colour would disguise the lack of substance to the potage. I wrapped my scarf over my cap, obscuring as much of my face as I could, tucked the hatchet through my waistband, and carried the cauldron out to the main room to hang it over the fire. The smoke from both the fire and an assortment of clay pipes was filling the air nicely. I closed the flue some more, encouraging the smoke further, before throwing in the last of the dung. Glancing over my shoulder to be sure no one was watching, I slipped the tinderbox into my pocket.

Sauvegarde wandered over to cast a casual eye in the pot. His perfume choked me, even through the fug of smoke.

"What fare have you for us, my dear? That looks like stone soup."

"S'all we have, monsegnur," I mumbled in my best approximation of a southern accent. I pulled the hatchet out of my skirt and hefted it meaningfully. "Need wood." I hoped I sounded simple.

He leaned over me. "Don't do anything stupid, my sweet," he murmured into the top of my head. "Your father was just shot, trying to run."

My stomach heaved, and I felt bile crawl up my throat at the awful nearness of him. I didn't respond—just made my steadfast way to the door. I paused once I'd closed it behind me, gasping in great lungfuls of fresh air before heading into the stable yard.

Piles of hay had been scattered for the half-dozen horses who had joined Babette. None was tethered in the barn, which was good, and none of the men occupied the yard, which was better.

I hitched Babette to her cart, arguing with her while I pulled her away from the hay, and then cracked open the yard gate just enough to let a wily donkey see the way out. I half thought about bridling one of the fine horses grazing around me, but I knew I hadn't the skill to handle one. I withdrew the rapier from the back of the haystack, then, crouching in the far corner of the shed, sparked the flint into the dry fodder.

The bent old man hadn't been trying to escape. He'd said he was lighting a beacon. I didn't know who he would have signalled or what sort of beacon it would have been, but this would surely signal someone … someone who could be no worse than Sauvegarde.

It took multiple tries to start a flame, and several agonizing minutes coaching it, while I feared each moment that one of Sauvegarde's men would walk in. At last the fire took hold, and I retreated to the far side of the yard. Babette, who had returned to the haystack, lifted her head, snorted, and brayed a warning. I didn't know how smart the horses would be, but I knew Babette wouldn't stay in a burning barn. She backed out of the barn and into the yard, bumping into one of the horses with her cart, which caused him to aim a kick that missed both her and the cart. I nudged open the yard gate a little more, creating an invitation. Babette saw it and galloped toward it, blasting both doors open with the cart.

Fortune smiled, and the sentry who had come to investigate the noise received the gate full in the face. The horses thundered out behind Babette and were streaming past her in all directions. The sentry, reeling and clutching his nose, tried to run after them, but I swung the gate again, throwing my shoulder into it, then swung the back of the hatchet into the side of his knee for good measure. I ran in the opposite direction from most of the horses, hiding behind the carriage as men began pouring out of the inn.

I recognized my error too late as I saw Louis-Auguste and Étier dash towards the carriage—no doubt for weapons or valuables left inside. I ran, but not before smashing several of the spokes on the nearest wheel with my hatchet.

The month I'd spent on the road had restored the physical condition I'd lost wearing panniers and corsets at Versailles, but I couldn't hope to outrun two men, hampered as I was by skirts and a too-long rapier. I flattened myself behind the corner of the stable yard wall and waited, the rapier braced like a spear for whatever might follow.

There was no safety here, aside from that afforded by dark and lack of a sightline. Would Étier have his pistols primed? And what was the greater danger, his pistols or Louis-Auguste's sword? The former would be best to encounter close and soon, before the match was lit. The latter I wanted to stay as far away from as possible. But which would round the corner first?

These many thoughts went through my head in four quick heartbeats before I was answered. The long muzzle of a horse pistol extended past the corner into the moonlight, the arm that held it still protected by the wall. I ducked, curling like a sow bug over the hilt of the rapier I carried. The blade of Louis-Auguste's sword appeared above my head, and his foot advanced in front of my eyes. It took only the slightest reach to extend my own blade between his legs. He tumbled forward, tripping on the sword and falling away. Only the fortunate fact I had both hands on the hilt kept it from ripping out of my grasp.

It pulled me with it, and I fell forward in front of Étier. I rolled towards him, hoping he would not fire so close to his own feet. This landed me on my back, staring up into Étier's shadowed face and the barrel of both pistols. He, too, thought better of firing so close and dropped one weapon on the ground to better reach down and make a grab for my rapier hilt. The impact must have hit the flint to the pan, for there was a deafening bang and a spray of dirt and stones that peppered the side of my face, half blinding me. It did the same to Étier, though, who reeled backward, clutching his face. This gave me the breath of time I needed. Thinking of Babette, I drew in my legs and shot them out, straight into Étier's knees.

I was no donkey, but panic fuelled my muscles. I heard a crack, and Étier doubled over, falling towards me. Instinct lifted my hands, one of which still held the rapier. There was a brief tremor as the blade hit resistance — a rib, I thought in a moment of clarity — before the blade skipped over bone passed through Étier's chest as he fell on me, crushing the air from my lungs.

I was imprisoned by his weight, unable to move, the horned pommel of the rapier like a spike in my own belly. And then he coughed, dousing my face in wet warmth that could be only blood. I heaved with all my fear-fuelled strength, feeling my own ribs twist and crack, till I wriggled out from beneath him, using my feet to push his limp body away at last.

I struggled upright, using the bloodied rapier as a crutch while I looked for Louis-Auguste. He was back on his feet as well, but without his sword. It lay a few paces behind him, glinting in the light of the low-hanging moon. He gripped his right arm in his left, a dark stain seeping between his fingers. He stared at Étier, at the pistol that lay on the ground, at me.

I couldn't have wounded him when I tripped him. Did Étier's ball hit him? It didn't matter—he lunged for the expended weapon while I clawed at the other still caught in Étier's dead hand. I lifted the massive horse pistol, my arm trembling under its weight. I had no idea whether it was cocked, or even how to fire it. However, as Louis-Auguste pointed the weapon's twin at me, I knew one thing.

"That one has been discharged," I said. "This still has a ball and powder."

"Do you know that for sure, mademoiselle?" he challenged, bold as brass.

"I am willing to wager," I said, stepping over Étier's corpse without taking my eye, or my aim, off Louis-Auguste. I circled slowly, giving him a wide berth. "I have a firearm that may or may not be loaded, but you have one that definitely is not." With my left hand I raised the sword, pointing its wobbling tip at him. "And I have this."

As I backed away my heel struck something—his fallen sword. Keeping the pistol aimed at him, I stuck the bloodied rapier through my apron's waistband and bent, picking up the other. Two swords and a pistol formed a considerable encumbrance, but I couldn't risk leaving him with any of them. By now

I had reached the edge of the stable yard where the scrub oak began. I backed into it, ignoring the prickles that clawed at my skin, until I had disappeared into the brush.

I waited a few breathless moments, crouched in the scrub oak, trembling like a rabbit beneath the gaze of a hawk, sure the sound of my hammering heart could be heard for leagues. But there was far too much other noise now: the shrieking roar as fire engulfed the barn, the shouting of men, and the fracas of panicking horses.

I lifted a cautious eye above the dense prickles but saw no sign that Louis-Auguste, or anyone else for that matter, had followed me into the scrub. The men milling in the yard were no more than black shapes against the fire. An eruption of flames and tufts of burning hay burst into the air like the fireworks of Versailles, raining down on the men and the carriage.

Babette. Where was Babette? I stood to peer up and down the road. The moon had set, and the sky was greying at the corners, but it was still too dark to see which way she might have fled. A stray sheep would head to the last place there was good forage, and Babette was smarter than a sheep, so I cast my die and hoped she would aim herself back up the road we had come down.

Moving with any speed within the scrub was impossible, so I ventured back to the edges and followed the verge as best I could, crouched to keep my silhouetted head from showing. It was slow going, tripping over rocks and roots, tearing my hair and face with branches when I strayed too close to the prickly scrub. The two unsheathed rapiers in my apron poked me in the sides and dragged in the dirt as I went, and the flintlock weighed on my bruised ribs and arm. I dared not thrust it through my waistband along with the two swords and the hatchet, for it still seemed to be cocked, and I wasn't sure how to disarm it, short of firing. I placed it deep within the branches of a prickly oak and hoped that weather would damp the powder before a hapless sheep or shepherd happened upon it.

I cursed Luc for abandoning me and hoped he hadn't fallen afoul of Sauvegarde's crew already. For all I knew, Luc was dead in a ditch by the time I'd been rudely awoken by the arquebusier. And Jacques. For he wouldn't have run off if Luc had been attacked. I shook foolish tears out of my eyes. There was no sense crying over a lost lamb until you saw a carcass. All I had left for certain was Babette, so I had to find her.

At last I saw her white rump glowing in the half-light of dawn. She was chewing dry grass by the side of the road, muzzle to muzzle with one of the fine beasts I'd freed from the stable yard. I scrambled down the bank and threw my arms around her neck. The horse snorted and shied away, but Babette stood there chewing contentedly as I buried my face in her short brush of a mane. She was leaning down for another bite when her neck tensed and her head shot up, enormous ears swivelling forward.

I dropped to my haunches. A voice came from the darkness. "Stand away."

I stood slowly, allowing my cloak to cover the rapier guards on either hip. A huge shadow moved onto the road. There was a sudden spark of flint followed by the glow of a match.

"Sir," I said in my lightest country voice, reaching beneath my cloak for the handle of a rapier. "I have no valuables. There is a fire at the inn——" I continued, as if any fool could not see it.

"Drop the swords. And the pretence," came the voice.

I drew Sauvegarde's rapier from my left side and tossed it to the ground, keeping my cloak over Louis-Auguste's sword on my right. "Let me go on my way, sir," I said without the southern accent, "and I'll allow you the same."

"And the other one," he said.

I let Louis-Auguste's rapier fall to the ground beside his friend's. At least I still had the hatchet tucked into the back of my waistband.

"Step over there." He motioned me away from Babette. "And remove your cloak."

I complied, wishing I'd kept the pistol and watching as the man, now silhouetted by the light of the blaze, picked up both rapiers and tossed them in Babette's cart. The matchlock stayed trained on me the whole time.

"Right. Lift your skirts. To the knee is fine." As I complied, he grabbed my elbow, spun me around and snatched the axe from my back. It went into the cart too. He drew a lace from his shirt. "Hold this." I didn't dare disobey with the firearm's baleful eye still lit, so I grasped the string. "Hands together, behind your back, wrists touching." In short order my hands were bound.

He pinched out the matchlock and gagged me with a kerchief that smelled all too familiar. I knew the shape, the voice, and now the scent of my accoster, but it wasn't yet clear he knew me.

He escorted me off the side of the road, where I stumbled in a dry ditch and went to my knees. Only his hand on my elbow kept me from falling entirely. He dragged me to my feet, and through a gap in the scrub, but my eyes lingered on the unexpected and cheerful sight of yellow primulas glowing in the muted light. It was a lonely patch, incongruent in the winter-dry grass.

To my astonishment, on the other side of the prickly windbreak, a well-tended road seemed to wind through the umbrella pines. My captor lashed my hands to a tree and then disappeared through the gap in the scrub. He was back minutes later with Babette in tow and the horse following of its own accord. I was unlashed from the tree but not ungagged. Had I been, I would have shouted at the idiot.

"Get in," he said, pointing at the cart.

When I only glared at him, he added, "Or I'll bundle you in like a load of washing."

I half turned away and lifted my elbows, indicating my tied hands. Instead of taking this as a suggestion to unbind me, he picked me up under the arms and swung me in.

I landed on the quillons of one of the swords and cursed him as best I could with the gag in my mouth. He ignored me and led Babette away, jolting me on the ruts of the road.

Imbecile, I raged behind the gag.

I shifted in the cart, lifting my buttock from the offending rapier guard. I hooked the hilt with two fingers and inched forward to brace the sword against the side of the cart with my hip. From this awkward position, I ran my tied wrists against the blade, slowly sawing through the cord that bound me, interrupted each time the cart hit a rut. The blade was not particularly sharp in its middle, though I managed to nick myself more than once. I inched further along until I felt the cord catch on a burr in the steel. That gave me resistance, and I worked my hands faster, fretting with awkward tugs against the tiny imperfection.

The cart turned right at a Y in the trail, and we passed another group of buttery primulas. These could be no coincidence. Someone had planted them.

I was distracted from that line of reckoning when the cord about my wrists gave way at last. I cut myself in earnest this time, the blade sinking into the heel of my hand.

I wrenched the kerchief from my face and pressed the filthy thing against my bleeding hand. My captor's back was still to me as he walked beside Babette. I could jump from the cart and run before he noticed. Instead I picked up the less bloody rapier, leaned forward from the cart, and swatted him on the shoulder with the flat of the blade.

"Henri, you idiot," I said. "Unhand my ass."

He turned more quickly and smoothly than a man his size ought to be able, and he wrapped his arm around the blade of the sword, rendering it harmless, enveloped as it was in the thick fabric of his sleeve and held snug against his body. "Bonjour, mademoiselle."

A slight upward twist from him and the handle of the sword slipped from my bloody hand—wrenching my fingers along the way. Furious, I reached for the other rapier at my feet, but his hand came down on top of mine, bringing his face far too close to mine.

"Ah, ah, what did I ever do to you, Toinette?" He tossed aside the first rapier then used his massive hand to pry the other sword from my fingers and remove it from the cart as well.

"Aside from trussing me like a *pintade* and tossing me in my own cart?" I spat. I still had the hatchet, but was not fool enough to reach for that.

"How was I to know it was you?" he said with an innocent shrug. "Though it's true; every other time I've met a girl with a cart on the road late at night, it has been you." He cocked his head sideways. "At least this cart has a donkey." He held out a hand. "Would you care to walk or ride the rest of the way?"

"The rest of the way where?" I asked.

"Well, I believe I found two friends of yours," he said as I reluctantly accepted the hand down. "Just a little farther along the trail of yellow roses."

§

Find out what lies at the end of the primose path in Pulp Literature *Issue 40, Autumn 2023.*

the adventures of Allaigna sing

simply a joy to read

Allaigna's Song
Overture
AMAZON #1 BESTSELLER
JM Landels

Allaigna's Song
Aria
JM Landels

keeps you turning pages from beginning to end

An immensely satisfying epic

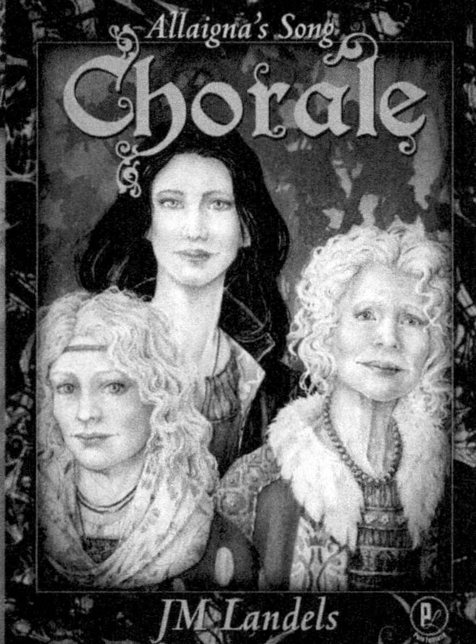

PULPLITERATURE.COM/ALLAIGNAS-SONG/

THE ARTISTS

M St James

Cover artist, Ups and Downs

Michelle St James is an author and artist living in the foothills of North Carolina. Originally from New England, she has traced her family's roots back to 1621 in Plymouth, Massachusetts. After three decades of working in acrylic, oil, and pastel, she has embraced digital art with enthusiasm. Her work has appeared on recent covers of *Factor Four Magazine, Spaceports & Spidersilk, The Maul Magazine, ParSec, Diet Milk Magazine,* and *The Vampiricon,* among others.

Although creating art has always been a part of her life, the pandemic lockdowns allowed her to turn to it, and creative writing, full time. During the first three months she wrote a middle-grade mystery novel, *The Mermaid of Agawam Bay,* influenced by growing up on the south shore of Massachusetts.

Ups and Downs was inspired by the idea of a woman experiencing the end of a romantic relationship. The glass floor is sure to break under the weight of her heartbreak. She's cast the symbol of romantic love, the rose, aside, and discarded the love letters she'd been reading and answering, letting all reminders of her lover blow away with the wind. The raven is advising her "Nevermore," and the upended ink bottle ensures there will be no going back.

View M St James's digital art at stjames-art.com, and her works in oil, acrylic, and pastel at earthtonespaintings.webs.com.

Read selected stories for free at shellstjames.com. *The Mermaid of Agawam Bay* by Shell St James is available on Amazon.

ANAT RABKIN
Illustrator, 'Dragon's Greed'
Anat has been drawing since she was old enough to hold a pencil, and dreaming up stories even longer. She has been published in multiple issues of local comic anthologies by Cloudscape Comics Society. As well, Anat had a webcomic that was published twice a week for over four years, and she sold short comics at the Vancouver Comic Arts Festival (VANCAF). While self-taught in art, she did attend school for game design. When Anat is not creating elaborate stories, she is working on them as a game developer at her dream job. Her previous *Pulp Literature* appearances include 'Forbidden Fruit' (Issue 9), 'It Rained Then Too' (Issue 13), and 'For the Love of Grey' (Issue 17). She currently lives in Vancouver, British Columbia.

MEL ANASTASIOU
In-house illustrator
Mel Anastasiou loves drawing for *Pulp Literature* because she loves the stories she illustrates. She draws in black and white, working from imagination and inspired by details from Renaissance compositions. You can find illustrations, writing tips, and news about her books and novellas at melanastasiou.wordpress.com, and see more of her artwork on Facebook at Bird and Branch Artwork.

HALL OF FAME

These are the heroes — the Patrons and Pulp Literati whose monthly support helped bring you this issue. Please lift your glasses and give them a rousing cheer!

The Brewers
Robin McGillveray

The Landlords
Isabel Cushey
Dana Tye Rally
Adam Fout

The Innkeepers
Ada Maria Soto
Margot Landels
Ev Bishop
Susan Jackson
Kevin Harris
Gillian Gardiner
Richard Ohnemus

The Cicerones
Roger & Anne Anastasiou

The Bartenders
Alana Krider
Richard Gropp
Ron Graves
Kristen Mah
Victoria McAuley
Dave Wayne

Scott F Gray
Michelle Balfour
Abigail Bruce
Vernice Dietra Malik
Katriona Greenmoor
AD Bane
KT Wagner
Deepthi Atukorala
Margot Spronk
Margaret Elliott
Peter Halasz
Bjarne Hansen
Leny Wagner
Kain Stewart
Chris Olee
kc dyer
Kimberley Aslett
Jan Fagan
Brighton Hugg
Alexa Benzaid-
	Williams
Bryan Moose
Maureen Cooke
K Anastasiou
Mike Sylvester
Wichael Tellez
Katherine Derbyshire

Kerri Chamberlin
Rapscallion
Shannon Saunders
Megan Shaw
James Carlino

The Regulars
Marta Salek
Rina Piccolo
Jenny Blackford
Akemi Art
BC
Meredith Frazier
Catherine Levinson
Vera
Charity Tahmaseb
Marilyn Holt
Barbara Pengelly
David Perlmutter
Steve Mashburn
Christa Walker
Hannah McManus
Melissa Daniels
SR Harper
Paul Anguiano

If you would like to join the ranks of these worthies, you can become a patron on Patreon at patreon.com/pulplit or join the Pulp Literati through our website at pulpliterature.com/join-pulp-literati/.

Out of the fires of a Caribbean slave revolt, shipwrecked on the jungle coast of 16th-century Ecuador, an educated slave, a shaman, and a monk hunted by the Inquisition fight for freedom against the might of Imperial Spain.

Dive into an epic slipstream novel of intrigue and adventure from fantasy author Matthew Hughes, the writer George R.R. Martin calls 'criminally underrated,' and Robert J. Sawyer says is 'a towering talent.'

'A triumph!' - Cecelia Holland
'Sensational' - Candas Jane Dorsey

pulpliterature.com

Fantastic Fresh Fiction!

PULP *Literature*

Room Magazine

2022 Contest Calendar

Creative Non-Fiction
1st Prize: $1000 + publication
2nd Prize: $250 + publication
April 1 - June 15

Poetry
1st Prize: $1000 + publication
2nd Prize: $250 + publication
June 15 - August 31

Short Forms
1st Prize: $500 + publication
(two awarded)
September 1 - November 15

Covert Art
1st Prize: $500 + publication
2nd Prize: $50 + publication
November 15 - January 15, 2023

ROOM

Making Space in Literature, Art & Feminism Since 1975

Entry Fee: $35 (for entrants residing in Canada), $45 (for entrants residing in USA), $55 (for entrants residing anywhere else). Entry includes a one-year subscription to *Room*. Additional entries $7. Visit roommagazine.com/contest.

Do you have a **story to tell?**
We can help!

Dreamers is dedicated to heartfelt writing. Visit our site for:

- Therapeutic Writing
- Poems & Stories
- Content Marketing
- Creative Nonfiction
- Writing Workshops
- Contests & Anthologies
- Residencies & Retreats
- ...and so much more!

www.DreamersWriting.com

GEIST
go to geist.com/subscribe
or call 1-888-GEIST-EH
GEIST
BUS STOP NO PARKING
LOST CITY
Keep it weird.
Subscribe today!
FACT + FICTION ● NORTH of AMERICA

onspec
the canadian magazine of the fantastic
Expect the unexpected.
www.onspec.ca

MARCH 2022
MYSTERY MAGAZINE
All Original Stories
ORNTELLÀDAR
BY A.L. SIROIS
MARTIN HILL ORTIZ
JAZZ LAWLESS
DIANE A. HADAC
KYLE DECKER
JOHN M. FLOYD
MEHNAZ SAHIBZADA
JOSH TAYLOR
JOHN H. DROMEY
Try our
You-Solve-It
MYSTERY !

The Digest
Enthusiast
Book Fifteen C
January 2022
Tom Brinkmann
Steve Carper
Peter Enfantino
Stephen Jones
Gary Lovisi
Anthony Perconti
Jack Seabrook
David A Sutton

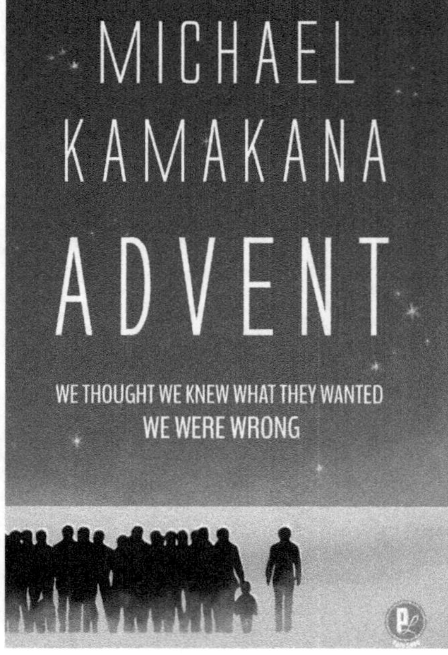

MICHAEL
KAMAKANA
ADVENT
WE THOUGHT WE KNEW WHAT THEY WANTED
WE WERE WRONG

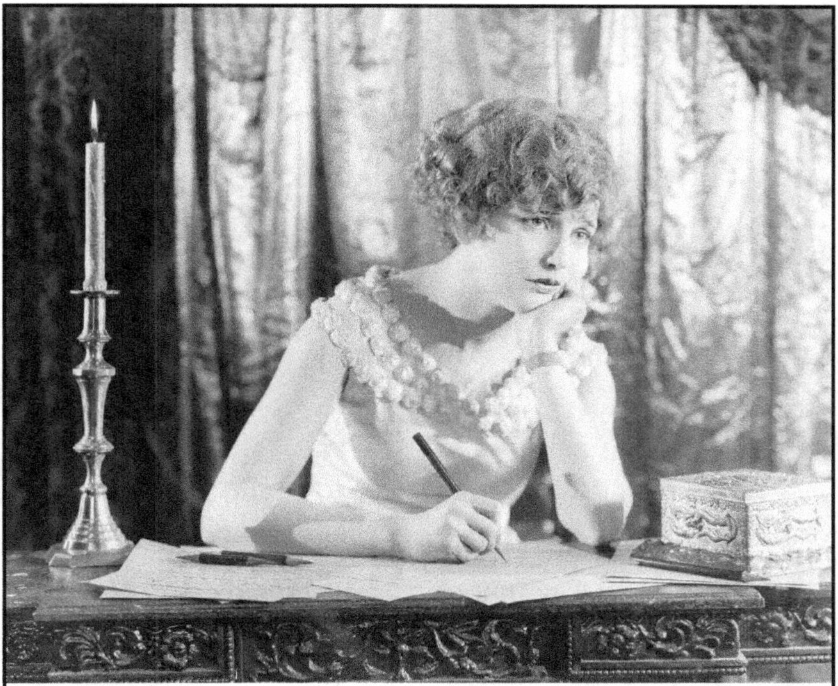

HELP WANTED?

If you are a new writer, or a writer with a troublesome manuscript,
EVENT's **Reading Service for Writers**
may be just what you need.

Manuscripts will be edited by one of EVENT's editors and receive an assessment of 700-1000 words, focusing on such aspects of craft as voice, structure, rhythm and point of view.

eventmagazine.ca

Port Coquitlam May Days

Readers & Writers Festival

A Tri-City Wordsmiths Event

Saturday May 6th, 2023

10am–5pm

Port Coquitlam Community Centre

2150 Wilson Ave.,

Port Coquitlam   kʷikʷəƛ̓əm

Workshops

Memoir * Journalism * Poetry * Mystery Writing
Publishing * Youth & Seniors

Blue Pencil sessions

Bookfair & Market Hall

Live readings & Open Mic

Arts & Writing Activities

TRI-CITY WORDSMITHS

tri-citywordsmiths.ca

MARKETPLACE

Books

Advent *by Michael Kamakana* • We thought we knew what the aliens wanted. Think again. • pulpliterature.com/advent

Allaigna's Song: Chorale *by JM Landels* The long-awaited conclusion to the bestselling *Allaigna's Song* trilogy. • pulpliterature.com/allaignas-song

The Extra: A Monument Studios Mystery *by Mel Anastasiou* • Extra Frankie Ray gets her big break on the Silver Screen, until Murder steals the scene. • pulpliterature. com/the-extra

The Labours of Mrs Stella Ryman: Further Fairmount Mysteries *by Mel Anastasiou* • Trapped in a down-at-the-heels care home. You'd be cranky too. • pulpliterature.com/stella-ryman-and-the-fairmount-manor-mysteries

What the Wind Brings *by Matthew Hughes* • Winner of the 2020 Endeavour Award • pulpliterature.com/product-category/novels/matthew-hughes

The Writer's Boon Companion *by Mel Anastasiou* • Thirty Days Towards an Extraordinary Volume • pulpliterature.com/subscribe/the-bookstore

Bookstores

Russell Books • 100-747 Fort St, Victoria, BC • russellbooks.com

Western Sky Books • 2132-2850 Shaughnessy St, Port Coquitlam, BC V3C 6K5 • 604-461-5602 • store.westernskybooks.com

White Dwarf / Dead Write Books • 3715 10th Ave W, Vancouver, BC V6R 2G5 • 604-228-8223 • whitedwarf@deadwrite.com

Conferences & Events

Port Coquitlam May Days Readers & Writers Festival • May 6, 2023 • Port Coquitlam Community Centre • www.tri-citywordsmiths.ca

Word on the Lake • May 2023 • Salmon Arm, BC • wordonthelakewritersfestival.com

When Words Collide • August 4–6, 2023 Calgary, AB • whenwordscollide.org

Wine Country Writers' Festival • September 2023 • winecountrywriters-festival.ca

Surrey International Writers' Conference October 2023 • siwc.ca

Printing & Publishing

First Choice Books/Victoria Bindery Book printing & binding • graphic design • eBooks • marketing materials 1-800-957-0561 • firstchoicebooks.ca

Magazines

Amazing Stories · Back in print! amazingstories.com

The Digest Enthusiast · Digests past & present plus new genre fiction larquepress.com

EVENT Magazine · Poetry & prose eventmagazine.ca

Geist Ideas + Culture · Made in Canada geist.com

Mystery Magazine · The cutting edge of short mystery fiction www.mysteryweekly.com

Neo-opsis · Canadian magazine of science fiction based in Victoria, BC · neo-opsis.ca

OnSpec · The Canadian magazine of the fantastic · onspecmag.wordpress.com

Polar Borealis · Paying market for new Canadian SF&F writers & artists · polarborealis.ca

Room Magazine · Literature, Art & Feminism since 1975 · roommagazine.com

Writing Resources

Dreamers Creative Writing · Workshops, residencies, contests & more! · www.dreamerswriting.com

Quit the Day Job · A school for writers from Pulp Literature Press pulpliterature.com/quit-the-day-job

The Writers' Lodge on Bowen Island The Muse retreats for writers · pulpliterature.com/calendar-of-events/retreats/

"A DAZZLING SLEUTH OPENS A NEW THRILLER SERIES!"

witty, heartwrenching, and heart-stopping

a fantastic read for mystery lovers!

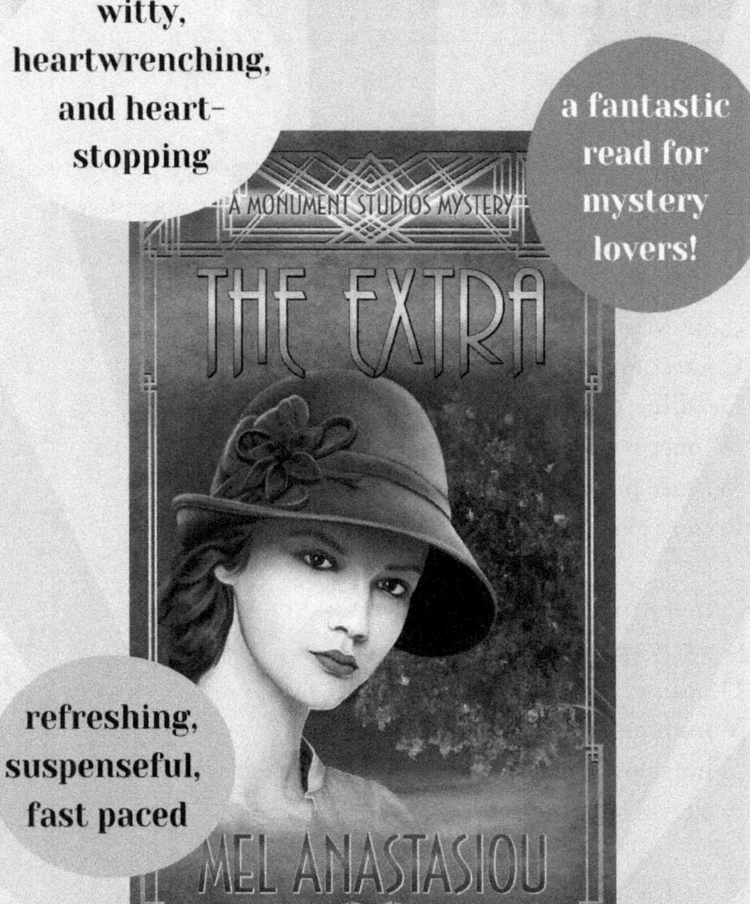

refreshing, suspenseful, fast paced

"The conjugal blend of mystery and Hollywood atmosphere works on every level. Very highly recommended."

PULPLITERATURE.COM/THE-EXTRA-A-MONUMENT-STUDIOS-MYSTERY

CONTESTS

Pulp Literature runs four annual contests for poetry, flash fiction, and short stories. For contest guidelines, prizes, and entry fees, see pulpliterature.com/contests.

The Magpie Award for Poetry
Contest opens: 1 March 2023
Deadline: 15 April 2023
Winner notified: 15 May 2023
Winner published: Issue 40, Autumn 2023
Prize: $500

The Hummingbird Flash Fiction Prize
Contest opens: 1 May 2023
Deadline: 15 June 2023
Winner notified: 15 July 2022
Winner published: Issue 41, Winter 2024
Prize: $300

The Raven Short Story Contest
Contest opens: 1 September 2023
Deadline: 15 October 2023
Winner notified: 15 November 2023
Winner published: Issue 42, Spring 2024
Prize: $300

The Bumblebee Flash Fiction Contest
Contest opens: 1 January 2024
Deadline: 15 February 2024
Winner notified: 15 March 2024
Winner published: Issue 43, Summer 2024
Prize: $300

ℬecome a Patron of Pulp Literature

By supporting *Pulp Literature* on Patreon with $2 or more per month, you will be laying the foundation for a secure future for the magazine, as well as ensuring that you never miss an issue! Your subscription includes four big issues of short stories, novellas, poetry, comics, and novel excerpts, delivered to your door or electronic mailbox each year. **Find us at patreon.com/pulplit**

If you prefer to subscribe through our website, go to pulpliterature. com/subscribe.

Or you can send a cheque with the form below to
Subscriptions, Pulp Literature Press, 21955 16 Ave, Langley BC, V2Z 1K5, Canada

❑ **Send me 2 years (8 issues) at the special rate of $90** (save $30)*
❑ **Send me 1 year (4 issues) for $50** (save $10)*
❑ **Send me 2 years of digital issues for $30** (save $9.92)
❑ **Send me 1 year of digital issues for $17.50** (save $2.47)

Name: ____

Address: ____

City: ___________________________ Prov. / State: _________

Postal code: _______________ Country:__________________

Email: ____

❑ Payment enclosed
❑ Bill me
❑ New
❑ Renewal

Make cheques payable in Canadian funds to Pulp Literature Press. Include email address for digital editions and Paypal billing, or subscribe at www.pulpliterature.com.

*for postage outside Canada add $20 per year in North America or $36 per year overseas.

www.ingramcontent.com/pod-product-compliance
Lightning Source LLC
Chambersburg PA
CBHW061302210726
48293CB00003B/1078